THE HYMN OF

MARA

Gregory T. Glading

ISBN

Hardcover: 978-1-970399-20-2

Paperback: 978-1-970399-19-6

The Hymn of Mara is Gregory T. Glading's eleventh novel. All
his works carry a Christian message, although not all are
scripturally accurate.   The Hymn of Mara, along with his novel,
Rivka's Revelation, are true Christian novels dedicated to the Lord
and true to scripture.

About the Author

The Hymn of Mara is Gregory T. Glading's eleventh novel. A Temple University graduate, the author served a combat deployment in Iraq with the 1-12 First Cavalry Division in 2003 and 2004, and was awarded the *Order of the Spur* among numerous medals. Gregory T. Glading has achieved the distinction of being among the few former professional athletes to have written multiple standalone, adult novels without a co-author, and possibly the only one to do so outside of the sports genre. He currently lives in Lakeland, FL, with his family, and is writing his latest novel titled *The Seventh Bell.* The story returns to the author to his South Philadelphia roots.

Acknowledgments

Writing The Hymn of Mara meant tackling a time, place, and culture that I had no prior experience, education, or knowledge of. It took considerable research, diligence, and prayer to complete this novel. I am confident in the results, thanks to the support of NYBP's executive liaison, Emma Becker; my editor, Sephora Vaz; the illustration team that brought my cover vision to life; and especially my production manager, Sophia Hudson, who oversaw the transformation of the rough manuscript into a book.

Table of Contents

Chapter 1

Seven thousand? Eight thousand? How many thousands of miles away from home? Engineer in Charge Lawrence Mills gazed at an Amur Falcon soaring overhead. *And that's if I were lucky as you and could fly it in a straight line, my feathered friend.* Lawrence continued to watch the bird soar toward the tourmaline horizon. *Even if I could fly like you…What would await me back in Philadelphia? I wish sprouting wings and escaping from this Assam ring of Dante's Inferno were that simple. The Indian British Raj…Regardless of how and why I got here, no matter the heartbreak and deception, I have a job to do. Yet Eight Thousand Miles,* Lawrence took off his American wide-brim felt hat, worn in defiance of a British pith helmet, and wiped sweat from his brow before tucking his survey map under his arm. *A couple of years ago, I read about Wilber Wright's flying contraption. It flew eight hundred feet…But you,* he watched the Amur Falcon vanish into the distance, can fly forever. *Here, I'm grounded. Seven weeks of steamships, ferries, and trains away from home. But the letter? It waited for me upon my arrival.* Lawrence lowered his head and pinched his nasal bone. *Maybe after I forget her, things will improve. The monsoon summer will end. It feels eternal, but they all assure me, sometimes with a laugh, that even here the season will change. I hope they're right. The Pennsylvania Winter has nothing on this damn Summer. What would I give for a little snow and ice? Even Hell can't top this place. The rich man begged Abraham to send Lazarus to dip the tip of his finger in water to cool his tongue.* Lawrence sniggered at himself. "I'll take some dryness right now. The mustiness and mold, the monsoon humidity and torrential rain, maybe the Hindus have a worse Hell than this. They'll have to convince me."

The clanging of native workers clearing a cut through the jungle's green undergrowth with machetes and axes flailing against bamboo and bracken overwhelmed the sawing of cicadas and the cooing of jungle birds. Lawrence pinched his chin. *Gone are Bucyrus steam shovels and excavators; present are elephants and oxen. American machinery can accomplish in days what takes weeks here. Even the Appalachian Mountains can't challenge the Assam jungle for harsh terrain. How do the workers survive? Barefoot and carrying baskets. Thinner than reeds. Their hard labor should make them look like Eugen Sandow.* He looked at one of four British soldiers providing security. *They resent me and don't like taking orders from an American civilian, but at least I have someone to talk to in English, and they're only here for security and deterrence, with no say in how the workers are treated. The natives have it bad enough. The last thing they need is an abusive overseer. The cut looks good. We have a job to do. The soldiers, the workers, and I are working together to get it done, and we're getting it done well.* A jungle flower broke the scent of dampness. A bitter-sweet aroma. *Dorothy Cabot...Loveliness and delight...Now deceit and betrayal.* Lawrence gritted his teeth before muttering aloud. "So, a solid family living on a leafy acre in Wayne wasn't good enough for the Cabots? The Haverford School and the University of Pennsylvania. What more could they ask for? Yet those top-notch schools failed to teach me a Mainline fact of life. The upper middle class can rub shoulders with old money, socialize, and even conduct business, but never gain acceptance as equals. Not last generation, this generation, or the next generation. And to think that our newspapers sometimes mock the British way of birth rather than merit. And the Indian caste system? They can learn a thing or two from Mr. George Cabot." Lawrence looked around. He was relieved to realize that the noise of elephants dragging away logs cloaked his talking to himself. *This racket, what a far cry from Beethoven's Third Symphony...*

...The Philadelphia Academy of Music... *Coattails, white tie, and top hat. So dapper I looked, yet Dorothy, your pompadour hairstyle, swept high from your forehead with light curls pinned on the back...You carried me away. I'm six feet tall.* Lawrence pinched his chin. *The crown of your hair topped my eyes.* He closed his eyes and tilted his head. *Those high cheekbones and your celestial nose dusted with rice powder... Your skin glowed in the gaslights, and a whisper of carmine on your full lips...Oh, how I wanted to, but I didn't dare kiss them. How can I ever forget taking your* white-gloved hand and helping you from the carriage? Your evening slippers, with just an inch or so of slender Louis heel, lifted your twinkling blue eyes just a tad below mine. Dorothy, your Edwardian gown with its floor-length ivory satin overlay with panels of pale champagne chiffon…You could make the goddesses and angels green with envy. Oh, how it subtly tantalized what was underneath. Yet no gown could match your elegance, posture, and poise. How sweeping back your shoulders enhanced your S-bend high-waisted bodice, helping you hold your bosom slightly forward, and your hips in a gentle counterpoise. Forget six feet tall, having you on my arm made me feel ten feet tall, and you would soon be my wife. Or so I thought.

A trumpeting elephant and a falling banyan tree broke his reverie. "Am I coming down with tropical fever? Get a grip on yourself. How long was my mind elsewhere? This place is fraught with danger. Be more alert, Lawrence. Besides, I've got a job to do, and getting sent home in a straitjacket won't suffice." Lawrence trotted his horse to the fallen banyan tree. The workers, without being told, had wrapped one end of a chain around it and attached the other end to an elephant. The elephant dragged it away. *That night, sitting in the Philadelphia Academy of Music with Dorothy…I would've volunteered for a straitjacket right then, and there if I thought just three months later, I would be supervising elephants…It wasn't my first visit to the Academy of Music. While my family was well-to-do and the Pennsylvania Railroad paid me well, it was my first time in a private box. I wished it weren't the Cabot box, and I wasn't sharing the evening with Dorothy's parents. Yet to hold her hand while she lowered into that red, plush velvet chair under crystal chandeliers. Yet its glitter played second fiddle to the gleam in her eyes.*

The musicians tuned their instruments in discordant tangles with the opening of the gold-fringed, heavy red velvet curtains. *I stood with the audience and clapped as the Philadelphia Orchestra's conductor, Fritz Scheel, took center stage. Yet it was Dorothy who was the silence before the strings.*

The audience sat while the orchestra played Beethoven's Third Symphony…A sweat bead stung Lawrence's right eye. He opened his canteen, moistened his handkerchief, and held it over his eye. After blinking and washing away the sweat and water from his eye, he wiped down his face…*George and Diana Cabot, along with Dorothy and me. We exited the Philadelphia Academy of Music into the cool, misty air. Within five minutes, their horse-drawn carriage pulled up to the curb. The trip to the Union League was only a block away, yet a grand entrance from their Landau carriage was expected.* The four sat in plush leather chairs in a mahogany-paneled private room. They sipped brandy from cut, crystal snifters. "Mr. Cabot, I thank you for the orchestra experience. This cognac is on me. The railroad has promoted me to chief terrain engineer." Lawrence raised his chin, "I can afford it." Dorothy squeezed his hand and smiled her approval.

"The orchestra played magnificently." Dorothy cooled herself with her lace hand fan. "And Mr. Scheel is a wonderful conductor. Our orchestra is lucky to have someone of his caliber."

"A Century ago, Beethoven's Third Symphony shocked the world. It broke all musical conventions and had political overtones. Now it is considered the foundation of romantic music." George shifted his attention to Lawrence. "My bank is a major financier of the Pennsylvania Railroad." George sipped his cognac. "I am not only privy to the railroad's executive secrets, but as my bank is a major financer, I have a say in policy. Word is that you're a young man on the rise. I can make you rise even higher. I have secured you the position of engineer-in-charge with the British in India, specifically with the Bengal-Assam Line. It's yours for the taking. It will pay three times what you're making here. I can guarantee that not only will your job with the Pennsylvania Railroad be waiting upon your return, but your experience will put you on the fast track to the executive suite."

Lawrence gazed into his fiancée's eyes before returning his attention to her father.

"You have expressed a desire to care for my daughter without my help. The money you save from your duties in the British Raj will provide the means for an appropriate house, and another promotion will go a long way toward enabling you to give Dorothy the better life that she's accustomed."

A trumpeting elephant snapped Lawrence back into the present. The workers shouted over one another, tugging at the reins in a frantic effort to control the oxen. A tiger had emerged from the thicket, her muscles taught and ready to pounce. Yet she seemed more curious than angry. Corporal Stanton raised his rifle and aimed. Lawrence reached over and grabbed the barrel. "Fire a warning shot first. She knows we see her, and she knows we're out of her striking range."

The Corporal glowered at him. Resentment for having to take orders from an American civilian was manifest in his eyes and expression. Yet being a good soldier, he fired into the air. The tiger fled. He turned to Lawrence, "I know your President Roosevelt is big on conservation. Yet there are things you need to learn about India and the Assam jungle. A tiger is not a little black bear stuck in a tree. It is a killing machine like no other. Once it gets a taste for human blood, it will take many lives before even the most skilled and experienced hunter can bring it down. In your country, the snakes warn you with a rattle before striking; here, some spit in your eyes and blind you without warning or reason. Let one bite you, and you're dead."

"I understand." Lawrence nodded. "But that tiger is a magnificent creation. She will now avoid humans. I am learning more about the Jungle's spirit by the day. I respect the job you must do, Corporal. I expect you to respect mine, too."

"Sirdar," Lawrence spoke to the native man in charge. "Give the workers a break. Also, let them know that they're out of danger."

The Sirdar wore a white cotton dhoti, kurta, and turban. He nodded and shouted to the workers in Assamese.

Chapter 2

The final minutes of Mara's last class of the day slipped by. Her thoughts turned to the church dispensary and her second vocation as a self-trained nurse. She taught her young students in English but would speak Assamese to a student who had difficulty with a lesson. Visiting British citizens chuckled at her hybrid Assamese and strangely accented English. She often shifted between English and Assamese when teaching scripture, wanting the message and interpretation to be understood both intellectually and culturally.

Her village of Sundarpur long ago had accepted her Assamese mother's marriage to an American missionary. Mara looked out of the classroom window. She closed her eyes and let her mind wander. *When can I visit the mysterious land of my father? The United States of America. I have listened to my father's tales, read about it in books, and often dreamt of it. America lacks a caste system and presents opportunities for women. Could I be a doctor if I lived in America? My father left his country to devote his life to serving God and his fellow man. What is God's ultimate purpose for me? I now joyfully sacrifice and serve. But I can do it better with more education. I wished to attend Bethane College in Calcutta, like my mother. Unfortunately, she says they would never accept me because of my mixed blood. She must be right. I have wrestled since childhood for acceptance from both the British and Assamese, and I know I will never belong to a caste. My father tells me that America would accept me. Yet Sundarpur needs me. They have more than accepted me. They have embraced me for my service to the village. I have worked hard homeschooling with my parents. My mother was a music major and is an excellent voice coach. She brought me sheet music from Gauhati and Calcutta, and my father taught me from many books. Books are my window to the outside world and give me the knowledge to serve as both a teacher and a nurse.*

Her physical beauty enhanced her aura of goodwill. Mara stood taller than most women in Sundarpur. Although she inherited her father's pale complexion, unrelenting sun exposure gave her skin a burnished luster. Mara boasted her mother's thick black hair, which flowed to her mid-back. Set a harmonious breadth apart, her luminous almond eyes gleamed rich brown with an earthy warmth. Her arched brows and feathered lashes lent her beauty a tender grace. Thin but not waifish, her movements were ethereal and elegant.

As her lesson ended, a twelve-year-old Assamese boy raised his hand. Mara smiled and pointed at him. "Yes, Arun."

"Thank you, Miss Mara, for teaching us English. But please, ma'am," He pressed his palms together and slightly bowed, "could you sing to us in our Assamese?"

An eleven-year-old girl stretched out her arm. "Miss Mara, please, Madam, I would like a song in English."

Mara smiled at her and walked over to a Broadwood and Sons upright piano sitting in the corner of the classroom. Its oak case was dulled by years of tropical damp, and its keys were yellowing, yet Mara treated it with love and care. While its thin, bright tone would never be mistaken for a grand piano, it combined with Mara's mid-soprano voice to serve as the children's ticket to another world. Mara sat by the piano and smiled at her class. "Arun wants to hear a song in Assamese. Padma would like one in English. How about I sing a song in German?"

The class politely cheered their approval.

"I know you won't understand the words, but music is a language even the Tower of Babel could not scatter. This song is by Franz Schubert. It's called Nacht und Traume. In English, that's Night and Dreams. In your language, it's rati aru sopon. 'Let the music comfort you as it tells you night is God's gift and in the quiet of our slumber, our dreams can rise like prayers."

The children sat still and quietly listened as Mara played the opening notes on the classroom piano. Mara's voice floated hushed and tender, like the mist carried by the nearby

Brahmaputra River on a westerly breeze. Her voice soon soared like a crystalline arc, leaving the children wide-eyed. Her singing echoed through the schoolhouse's wooden walls, making nearby villagers stop and listen.

After the children filed out of the classroom, Mara reached into her desk drawer and grabbed her brown, leather medical bag. She stepped from the schoolroom into the heavy afternoon sun and onto the packed-earth path to the mission clinic. Thrumming cicadas and cawing birds replaced children's voices. She glanced back at the Baptist Mission church and schoolhouse with its stone construction and corrugated tin roof. *It can never match the splendor of the great European cathedrals that I've seen in books. She* gazed at the ten-foot-high, rugged cross constructed from railway ties, *but is not humility the key to serving God? Our church and school serve the village's needs and allow us to teach God's word. But is it wrong to want to see, rather than just dream of, the great cathedrals or to listen to a symphony orchestra or opera and experience what man can achieve for God's glory? For is not beauty equal to truth and goodness? Here, God's creation abounds with beauty. His emerald trees and fronds, bamboo, and hibiscus flowers are a delight to my eyes and nose. I can only imagine the splendor of Paradise lost. Yet the serpents remain. Now they inject venom rather than tempt. I often see beautiful tiger and leopard skins. Yet their stealth has kept me from seeing them alive.*

The distant sound of the railroad construction: axes and machetes smashing trees, and the trumpeting and rumble of oxen and elephants, broke her reverie. *The Brahmaputra River is our lifeline. Steamboats bring us medical supplies and transport us to larger villages. Flooding, or shallow shoals during drought, make steamboat navigation difficult and dangerous, sometimes cutting us off from the outside world and denying us essentials. Many fear progress as an assault on tradition. I know the new railway will help our village and bring medicine that can leave Malaria and dysentery in the past.*

She wore a cotton blouse that covered her collarbone and was buttoned up to her neck. Its sleeves extended to her wrists, protecting her from the heat and mosquitoes. The hem of her cotton skirt draped over her brown leather sandals, sometimes brushing against the earth. A brown silken swath circled her waist, breaking the monotonous white. She wore a silver chain and cross over her chest, an heirloom from her grandmother. She placed her hand on her white scarf as a west wind blew in from the Brahmaputra.

Each day, the sound of railway construction gets closer and louder. The railway will make travel to Gauhati routine. The beauty of a Godly woman is what's on the inside. Yet I am often complimented on my outer beauty and told it's Heaven's gift. So, why is it wrong to want to look and feel more beautiful? When the railway is finished, I can go to Gauhati's markets far more often, experience its bustle, and shop for fashionable clothing. Must I always wear white? Mara pictured herself dressed in a lavender blue gown sewn from fine silk satin. Her long skirt was pleated and paneled, allowing it to sway with each graceful and elegant step. Mara brushed her hand over her chest. *I am a grown woman now. Are they not God's art and part of a woman's glory? Did not the Song of Solomon sing of their glory, like twin fawns feeding on lilies? I would look more beautiful than even the most elegant Englishwoman if my gown had an S-curved corset. Would holding my chest and hips forward just enough for proper admiration be a sin? Why is my mother fearful that a hint of feminine beauty would create sinful temptation as well as scandal and lies? I wish that she would know that outer beauty does not detract from inner beauty. Would Apostle Paul permit a modest pearl necklace or a gold bracelet? Oh, but I wish, just once, to wear a pearl necklace and emerald earrings like England's Queen Alexandra. Can I not have my long hair styled while maintaining decorum? I can bring back scented soap, perfume, and powders from Calcutta. Would not God want me to smell like a woman and not a railway worker or laborer on Sir Nigel's tea plantation? I gave my heart to my Lord Jesus. Yet I know my desire for a man is natural. Marriage is not forbidden. How can I find a good husband if he is not drawn to me as a woman? I will never find a suitable mate here in Sundarpur. Maybe the new railway can bring me to a tall and handsome Assamese man, or a British gentleman. My mother met and married an American. A Yankee, as the British call them. Maybe a Yankee is in my future. A future that doesn't exist in Sundarpur. How I wish to serve my God as a mother and raise my children to glorify him. God can bless me with a son or daughter who can transform our little schoolhouse into a university or our clinic into a hospital. Maybe my son or daughter can win many souls for Christ. How long must I wait?* She pictured herself on the arm of a tall gentleman wearing coattails and a top hat. He escorted her into a grand theater. *And my voice. I know it's a gift from God. My mother has trained me well, but even she says that a more experienced and accomplished teacher can make my voice glorify God even higher. Is staying in this village the same as my talent being a candlestick hidden under a bed, or burying it in the sand and expecting it to increase? The railway can allow me to serve my village and…*

A child's wailing ended her daydream. Mara jogged into the clinic. The child's mother was in tears. Sweat rained from her toddler boy's forehead and cheeks. Mara put her hand on his forehead. "I don't believe he has malaria, but he has a high fever." Maria walked over to a medicine cabinet. She mixed quinine powder into sweetened rice water. "Hold Haren's hand. He may reject this. I did all I could to make it taste less unpleasant, but he may try to spit it out. For that reason, and others, we must pray. Let us link hands." The three linked hands. Mara prayed. "Lord, it is written that when two or more are gathered in thy name, you are there. We ask that your name be glorified by blessing this medicine to little Haren's body and that you protect him and heal him." Haren's mother and Mara said, "Amen." Mara, in a fluid motion, put the spoon into Haren's mouth. He pulled his face in disgust. Nevertheless, he swallowed the quinine mixture. His mother at last smiled.

"Mrs. Sarma, I want you to stay in prayer. I feel comforted by the Holy Spirit that Haren will be fine. I will let you stay here with him. I want him to stay here in a well-ventilated room under a punkah fan and mosquito netting. I will have a punkah-wallah keep it in motion. God has put Haren in my hands. He is dehydrated. I have chemically treated water for him."

"Thank you so much, Miss Mara." Mrs. Sarma pressed her palms together at her chest and bowed her head. "You know that my husband and many in Sundarpur believe in multiple gods. But you have shown me that yours is the only God that loves us."

Chapter 3

Nigel Browning's high-boned face seemed carved from white marble. His piercing eyes were like oval chips of black onyx, fixed a micro-millimeter closer than a breadth apart. He cut his silver-tipped black hair with patrician precision. Standing tall enough for his shoulders to reach his horse's withers, his lean and proportionate body fit into his tailored white linen Edwardian riding attire as naturally as a second skin. Mounting his horse gave him an eagle's gaze. He tipped the visor of his pith helmet and made a sweeping survey of his tea plantation.

His fields stretched in endless green ranks like soldiers marching in rows over level ground, soon to venture over gentle hillsides and misty valleys. From his elevated view, his fields made him think of an Oriental emperor's garden. *The sweat and toil of my laborers and the profits from their wicker baskets of fresh-cut leaves make this possible, but it never happens unless my presence strikes fear.* Nigel looked upward. *Even the mynahs circling above seem to turn their wings aside. My laborers are not slaves or indentured servants. I need not crack a whip to keep discipline and order. Beyond my wages making the difference between their living or dying of starvation, it's my presence that commands their near worship and unswerving loyalty.*

Nigel Browning rode over to the western edge of his fields. A cut through the dense forest ran parallel to the construction of his new factory and warehouse. He had purchased more acreage in anticipation of an increased demand for its production. *The British government passed wasteland rules in my favor. The jungle is mine to clear by slashing and burning for tea cultivation. It's up to me to stop its relentless growth from reclaiming productive fields. My workers' fear of the jungle's tigers, leopards, and snakes distracts them from their duties. But they know my rifle and my superior wit have tamed the tigers and leopards, and that my boots trample the snakes underfoot.*

Nigel Browning remained on horseback and observed artisans placing a corrugated iron roof over a new brick processing plant with rows of long windows and slatted vents for ventilation and airflow. As soon as the roof was complete, he would have large wooden withering troughs, rollers to cut leaves, brass drying pans, and coal-powered fitting rooms. He would need to recruit additional skilled workers from Gauhati to make the increased production possible. Also running parallel to the freshly cut path was a new, windowless godown warehouse. Its teak beams, high ceilings, and plank floors were already installed.

Nigel smiled upon hearing the first rhythmic thud of hooves at the beginning of his clearing. A quarter of an hour later, he heard the drumming of iron-shod hooves, chains jangling, and leather creaking. The snap of a coach whip cut the morning air. Nigel stiffened, head tilting for his first view of the gleaming black landau carriage, drawn by four black horses and flanked by a mounted escort. Fredrick Robert Upcott, Chairman of the Railway Board, had arrived.

Nigel rode his horse on a slow four-beat gait to the Syce. "No need for the chairman to disembark here. Follow me to my manor." Nigel Browning trotted ahead of the Chairman's carriage and entourage over a gravel and packed-earth drive lined with banyan trees. He led them through a stone gate to his whitewashed manor rising above the tea fields like an Edwardian fortress. Built on a raised plinth circled with colonnaded verandas, it had tall, shuddered sash windows and a high-pitched, gabled roof extended with wide eaves. They stopped under a portico of Corinthian columns.

The Syce assisted Chairman Upcott from the carriage. Nigel Browning waited until the Chairman fully descended from the Landau before acknowledging him. The chairman had to straighten his posture and shift his weight to his toes to look up at the sturdy yet slender, imposing figure of Nigel Browning. Nigel slightly inclined his head before firmly shaking the Chairman's hand and holding it a measure longer than the Chairman expected. "Your presence alone brings honor to my estate. Would you further honor me by following me inside?" Nigel Browning snapped his fingers.

Servants scurried over and fanned the Chairman and his entourage. They entered the manor's great hall. Hunting trophies of tigers, leopards, and horned antelopes impressed as a sentry. Framed hunting rifles were on display. Nigel noticed Chairman Upcott staring into a mounted tiger's glass eye. "Is there a more formidable beast anywhere in the empire equal to a tiger? Or a creature as clever as the leopard? Yet neither can match my wits and rifles. The beasts of the jungle know who rules Assam. We even make the mighty elephant clear his own habitat. Here on my estate, civilization takes root in what was once savage soil. But men such as yourself tame India for the empire by laying iron veins for your fiery dragons of the rails."

They entered the drawing room. "Sit." Sir Nigel remained standing. He motioned to a plush, high-backed chair with lion heads carved on the armrests and lion claws on the feet. Four identical chairs were positioned around a low table placed above a multipatterned Persian carpet.

"You are a gentry's son." Fredrick Upcott sat. He glanced at Sir Nigel's reflection on a huge, wall-mounted gilt-framed mirror towering over him and turned away. Chairman Upcott wiped sweat from his bald pate despite sitting under churning punkah fans. "You did well to earn your inherited title, Sir Nigel. Your estate is impressive indeed. I can tell that the path my carriage traversed was freshly cut."

Sir Nigel sat silent for five taut seconds before snapping his fingers. "I apologize for the delay. Refreshments are arriving. The gentle jingling of ankle bells signaled the arrival of two barefooted female servants. They wore identical saris, although one was green sashed and the other red. Its silk clung to their lithe figures. Long, brown hair adorned with hibiscus flowers topped their even, delicate faces. The sweet aroma of lilac perfumed their smooth skin.

Chairman Upcott licked his lips at the sight of them.

One had a silver platter with tea in porcelain cups on top of saucers. The other bought a vine-embroidered China plate of prawn toast and curried chicken patties. A bead of sweat dripped down the chairman's face as they placed their trays on the table closest to him.

The female servants bowed to Sir Nigel and his guest. Nigel snapped his fingers. The servants, without turning their backs, retreated seven paces. They stood upright, hands folded at their waists, and their eyes cast downward. Sir Nigel finally sat. He reclined with calculated ease, one leg crossed over the other, and lightly drummed his armrest with taut fingers.

"Your hospitality, Sir Nigel, would impress royalty. Your fine tea and refreshments are exquisite. Your staff could work in Windsor itself."

"I handpicked my female servants from Calcutta. I freed them from their reeking bustee slum, their raggedy clothes, and malnutrition. Through discipline and guidance, I've refined them into ladies worthy of English society. My protection has allowed them to awaken to their full feminine glory. They are uncorrupted by so much as a single masculine hormone. I can read a man like a book. I can tell that you find them a delight."

Chairman Upcott gasped and wiped sweat from his brow.

"No need to speak, Chairman," Sir Nigel steepled his hands with fingertips touching, "It's that obvious. Nevertheless, if you didn't find them attractive, I would think less of you as a man. Their lives are held at my whim. The whip can enforce obedience, but it can never win loyalty. My subjects, whether house servants, artisans, or common labor, see me as more than a man. They see me as a figure of justice and power while never forgetting that I can decide who lives and dies."

"Yes. That may work for your plantation." Chairman Upcott placed his ankle over his knee. "But empire? No matter how much the people benefit from our presence, nationalism rules. Even with our advanced weaponry and iron fist, the people are still prone to rebellion."

"I don't want to question the king. Nevertheless, converting them to our culture is feckless. Rather, we exploit their ways. The Anglican Church has the Bishop of Canterbury, Randal Thomas Davidson, as primate of England. Pope Pius X leads the Catholic Church. The Muslim minority here has its Imams. The Jewish community esteems its rabbis. Yet they all look to a singular, supreme supernatural authority, and they have their Holy scriptures. I find it easier to control people who worship multiple Gods. To the Christians, the Lord is God himself. We designate Lord as a title. What if I could be Lord over more than this domain? What if they feared British rule as part of their divine order?"

"What are you saying?" Fredrick Upton raised his hands.

"Did the Anglican God prevent my beloved Theresa from dying while giving birth to a stillborn son? I built a Hindu Temple. The Hindus have their Gurus and Swamis, yet, not unlike the Protestants and Catholics, they have many divisions. Could we not avoid rebellion if we create a sect that reveres us as deities? My first loyalty is to King Edward VII and the empire. You and I are civilized, but if not for our rule, these people would remain savages."

"I think you're being too harsh."

"Harsh? Did I not say that I seldom need the crack of a whip or bang of a rifle to control? The deputy commissioner has already granted me additional land under wasteland rules. My plantation will soon extend to the Brahmaputra River. My new land will also flank the Bengal-Assam Railway Line. The path I cleared is only preliminary to a spur linking my processing plant and warehouse to the Bengal-Assam mainline. Yet it serves as only a suggestion. You, sir, have the authority to make that happen. Do so, and we all benefit."

"Building a spur to service a privately owned enterprise is seldom done." Upcott folded his hands in front of him and raised his lips in a thin crescent. "But not unheard of. You do understand that my position as Chairman of the Railway Board grants me tremendous power on all railway matters." Robert Fredrick Upton wiped sweat from his brow before swiveling his head from side to side. "You would not have called me here if building a spur to your tea plantation would not increase your profits by leaps and bounds."

"And investing in a spur to my plantation will also increase profits for the King's railway."

"The difference between you and me is that the Bengal-Assam railway line's bottom line does not affect my status."

"I anticipated your response." Nigel folded his hands behind his head. "I already know your information and have prepared a draft for my banker in England." Nigel Browning slid the chairman a folded paper slip. "I can personally assure his utmost discretion."

Mr. Upton opened the note and beamed. "I will have you meet with my Engineer in Charge, Lawrence Mills. He's a Yankee. Americans are uncultured and crass, but they are building an impressive nation. He held the same title with the Pennsylvania Railroad. I can assure you that he's the best at what he does. George Cabot recommended him to us. Mr. Mills will turn your cut into a railroad spur."

"Ahh, yes, George Cabot. Bankers of his eminence threaten to shift the world's financial axis from London to New York. It's better to stand beside men like George Cabot than stand in their way. I was informed of Lawrence Mills's qualifications." Nigel and Frederick shook hands. "I look forward to meeting Mr. Mills personally."

Chapter 4

Lawrence lowered the brim of his felt hat and shielded his eyes from the glare of the setting sun. The cicadas greeted the evening by swelling their chorus to a crescendo. He turned to the sirdar. "That's it for the day. Dismiss the workers."

The sirdar blasted his Pepa horn (Made from the horn of a buffalo with a bamboo reed mouthpiece) before shouting to the workers in Assamese. Some workers headed down the cut to their railway labor camp. Most walked ahead along a footpath to their home village of Sundarpur. Corporal Stanton rode over to Lawrence. "For a Yankee, Mr. Mills, you're not so bad. You do your job, and you do it well, while letting others do their jobs."

"The final horn just blew. We're off duty. I'm not in the British military, so calling me Lawrence works for me." Lawrence chuckled. "Still, I respect that you're a soldier. Do you prefer Corporal Stanton or your first name? Here we've worked together for weeks that seem like decades, and yet I don't know your first name."

"It's Douglas." Corporal Stanton smiled. "We're temporarily billeted in a government Dak Bungalow in Sundarpur rather than the military cantonment in Guahati. The cantonment has better food and drink, but at the Dak, we don't have to deal with senior officers watching our every move or ordering us around just because they can. Neither can match your engineer quarters. Yet Sundarpur is much closer, and it's getting dark, so why not follow me? Indian sepoy guards keep order at the labor camp, and the workers from Sundarpur are on their own. Sepoy guards, as always, watch our work site and equipment while we're gone." The Corporal beamed. "That means I'm now off duty. Off duty means gin and tonic." Douglas laughed. "We drink it because the tonic prevents malaria."

Lawrence scanned the worksite before answering, "It is getting dark, and I don't know if that tiger I stopped you from shooting will be grateful, so, a night in Sundarpur it is."

***

The corporal and the engineer rode along Sundarpur's packed-earth main road. Their horse's iron shoes made a distinct clicking noise. The scent of smoke from wood and dung fires, cattle tethered in byres, and wandering goats dominated the air, although flashes of jaggery and jasmine incense provided some relief. Some Sundarpur villagers respectfully nodded to Corporal Stanton; others kept their heads down, while a brave few turned their backs to him. One military-aged male stared them down.

Corporal Stanton placed his hand on his sidearm and glowered back. Many of their women and children murmured and pointed at Lawrence Mills, who wore leather riding boots that he brought from Pennsylvania, civilian khaki pants, a white cotton shirt, and a wide-brimmed felt hat, contrasting with Corporal Stanton's regulation khaki service dress, consisting of a buttoned-up tunic and a leather belt with brass buckles. Puttees were wrapped around his lower legs, ending in polished ankle boots. He wore a Wolseley helmet. Moreover, he had a rifle slung across his back, a bayonet at his hip, and ammunition pouches. A mother had to hold back her ten-year-old son from running up for a closer look.

An elder walked to the center of the road and stood before them, leaning on a bamboo staff. His dhoti of sun-faded cloth hung loose about his ankles. A white shawl with a red stripe was draped on one shoulder. His deeply lined face and gray hair gleamed slightly in the dusk, but it was his sharp and steady eyes that told a story. "Greetings, Corporal Stanton and friend." He pressed his palms together and slightly bowed. "I can tell your friend is an American like our resident Baptist minister."

"Yes, Goanbura, he is an American."

The Goanbura smiled at Lawrence. "Sundarpur is honored with your presence."

"He is the Goanbura, the village elder." Corporal Stanton turned to Lawrence. "He speaks English and serves as a liaison between the Assamese and the British. He has earned both their respect and our respect."

After a few seconds of silence, a woman's voice of ethereal tone and hypnotic pitch singing Franz Schubert's Ava Maria floated through the village, bringing a halt to all activity.

"My goodness gracious." Lawrence Mills dismounted his horse. "I've never heard anything so beautiful, so utterly angelic, in my life, and I'm talking as an aficionado of the classical arts."

The Goanbura pointed to a stone building with a corrugated tin roof fronted by a cross made of railway ties. "She is Mara. Her father is American like you, while her mother is one of us. Mara also serves us as a nurse. She treats us with your medicine, but the villagers believe that it is her voice, a gift from both her God and from our Gods, that heals our sick."

Lawrence stared at the church in silence.

"Come along, Lawrence. The Dak is right ahead at the edge of town," Douglas Stanton pointed at a single-story white plastered brick building with a high sloping roof and wrap-around veranda. "I'll tell you all about Mara and more over some gin and tonics."

"Thank you, Goanbura," Lawrence mounted his horse. "You have made me feel welcome in your village. I promise to strive to justify your hospitality."

***

Lawrence and Douglas sat at a cane table on the veranda. Flickers of light from a kerosene lamp danced on their glasses of

21

gin and tonic. "It looks like we have the place to ourselves." Lawrence sipped from his glass.

"Ah, yes, a far cry from a London pub. It's a lonely man's refuge. Rather, loneliness than the company of high-ranking officers. You, as a civilian and Engineer in Charge, can never know how I relish this taste of freedom." He held up his glass of gin and tonic.

Lawrence stared at the warm yellow-orange glow of the kerosene flames dancing on his glass, and the rising bubbles turning the firelight into specks of gold. The unvarnished cane tables and chairs, and worn pine cabinets holding dusty bottles of whiskey, gin, and rum, drifted into a vision of the plush leather chairs and mahogany paneled walls of Philadelphia's Union League private room. Dorothy sipped Remy Martin Cognac from a crystal snifter. Her smooth cheeks had a reddish glow; her long neck exuded a dash of Fleur d'Italie perfume... *Dorothy, Dorothy, even if you betrayed me, I can't stop loving you...*

"Blimey, Lawrence? Are you still with us, mate?" Before Lawrence could answer. Douglas laughed. "I think I get it. Are you here to get over a woman? Why here and not the French Foreign Legion?"

"It's a long story?"

"It's a long night. No electricity, no wireless, and no gramophone. There's no ballroom or orchestra. I don't see any other Westerners here." Douglas chuckled. "We're the only entertainment, so I'm game for a long story."

"For starters," Lawrence sipped his gin and tonic, "It's not what you think."

"So, I'm not far off." He folded his hands behind his head. "Tell me about her."

"Our social structure in America is not as rigid as England's. Still," Lawrence inhaled deeply. "Her name was Dorothy. She was lovelier than a spring garden and stunning as a symphony's apotheosis."

"I sense a but coming."

"Even from our side of the ocean, social and economic boundaries exist."

"You seem well-to-do, and I can surely tell that you're well-educated. What could have been the problem?"

"Come on, pal, you should know better. Even in America, a huge gulf separates the lower upper class from the aristocracy. An acre and a five-bedroom house is not a hundred-acre estate with a mansion. Dorothy was a Cabot. Her father didn't consider my lineage worthy of his precious daughter." Lawrence downed his drink. "Her father tricked me into taking this post to keep me from her. I know she loved me." He shook his hands. "I know it, even if her letter was waiting for me when I arrived." Lawrence bit his lower lip. "Two different worlds she wrote. That's right, pal, two different worlds. I played by the Cabot's rules, but, evidently, that wasn't good enough." Lawrence bitterly laughed. "Now I'm in an even more different world." He held his glass out for the waiter to refill. "Tell me your story. Was it a woman?"

"Well, old chap. Women are a distant memory. Other than a nurse in a military hospital, there ain't any women in His Majesty's Indian Army. Relations with local women are frowned upon. So, here I am halfway across the world from my country, hearing about heartbreak from a man even farther from his country."

"Okay, if not because of a woman, what landed you here?"

"Well, I must say, a five-bedroom house on an acre? You compared it to a hundred-acre estate with a mansion. I dare say your accommodation beats my flat in South London by the same margin. Despite you being a civilian, and you got fancy schooling that I never got a chance at, we're both railroad men and, well, you're a proper gent, you are, and you're awe right by me, mate.

Before enlisting in the King's Army, I worked as a railroad fireman. Shoveling coal into a steam locomotive boiler paid okay and kept my muscles tight, but didn't bring much adventure. At least it didn't leave you in one place. But it was hotter than the worst of the Assam summer. I'll get to the point. I was drinkin' ale in a pub in the East End. A recruiting sergeant came in and promised steady pay and food. Most of all, adventure. The Indian Raj. Land of tigers, leopards, and elephants. Sunshine rather than endless fog. The Army considered my railroad experience and assigned me to the Bengal-Assam Railway. While it's a soldier's right to gripe, overall, I ain't complainin', even if I must take orders from a Yankee civilian." He laughed. "Of course, they didn't tell me about the monsoons and the heat, and the cobras and the vipers, and mosquitoes and leeches. They're far worse than any Yankee civilian." He again laughed. "Yet the pay they promised is decent, and I've never gone hungry."

"I can't imagine George Cabot suffering these conditions." Lawrence sniggered. "But now that we're relaxing over a drink, dare I say that maybe we should appreciate the beauty and adventure of this land? I've learned that living it and imagining it through a Rudyard Kipling novel are two different things."

"Too right, mate. I may have only been a railway fireman from South London and don't have fancy schooling letters after my name, but I could walk to the Deptford and Bermondsey library. I read Haggard, Kipling, and Conrad." Douglas sniggered. "I guess they set me up for the recruiting sergeant."

"I can't imagine a woman like my Dorothy or her mother lasting half a day in this place. So, tell me about the woman behind the beautiful voice we heard. Mara?"

"Ah, Mara. You fell in love with her through her voice alone, didn't ya mate?"

"Don't I wish. Anything to break Dorothy Cabot's spell."

"Mara is a different sort o' woman. She's not like anything you've ever met. You'll have to visit an art museum to get an idea of her beauty. Her face is a masterpiece. My father fancied himself as an artist. My old man tried to teach me his craft, but I never advanced further than drawing walking stick figures. Mara," Douglas closed his eyes, took a deep breath, and tilted his head back. "For starters, her face has that perfect oval that my dad stressed, slightly longer than wide, with cheekbones tapering to a curve as smooth as polished ivory. You're an engineer and a numbers man. I'm sure you could quantify her beauty, but as far as I'm concerned, she can only be drawn by the hand of God himself.   As the Goanbura told you, her father is an American Baptist missionary, and her mother is Assamese, making her unique beauty something you won't encounter in the United States, England, or India, for that matter. Her form is perfectly slender with seeming divine grace. Yet she wears no make-up and only dresses in white. Her air is of someone you not only dare not touch but not even think an improper thought of. Why don't you go to her church service this Sunday? At the very least, you will hear her sing. Maybe she will break Dorothy's spell."

"For a working man from South London without a university degree," Lawrence shook his head, "You described Mara better than any scholar. On top of that, are we going to church to worship God or this Mara?"

"You have a point. We must worship the creator and not his creation." Douglas sipped his drink. "Yet beauty inspires a man to rise above himself and to appreciate his creation. Scripture does say, 'no eye has seen, nor ear heard, nor the heart of man imagined what God has prepared for those who love him'."

"Well, I was raised Presbyterian. I recall a sermon that advised us not to neglect showing hospitality to strangers because we may unknowingly encounter an angel. This Mara can't be an actual angel. If she's like you describe, we'd know she's an angel." Lawrence laughed and cuffed Douglas's arm. "I will say that The

Wayne Presbyterian Church, with its celestially high, vaulted ceilings and almost transcendent stained-glass windows, comes as close to a European Cathedral as you will ever find. I would take it all in and imagine Heaven, and I learned their Bible lessons. Unfortunately, spiritual matters still don't resonate with me. Yeah, I need to find something. What do you say, friend? I'm game for us to go to Mara's church this Sunday?"

"When you said 'unfortunately', it sounds to me like you're still undecided. Here, our lives are at risk with every breath we take. Whether from a wild beast with teeth and claws like a tiger, or a seditionist with a dagger, a cobra or a viper, or a deadly virus or malaria, we need to seek God, cause our next breath could easily be our last. I hope Mara's service leads you there. Talk to her father. The Reverend Sutcliffe is a Yankee from Boston, although he's been here for so long, I doubt he can talk to you much about home across the Atlantic. In the meantime, people have been mysteriously disappearing. In addition to finding God, I suggest you start carrying a revolver."

Chapter 5

Mara dusted a golden candelabrum with a white cotton cloth before adjusting it at a 45-degree angle to the church's hardwood pews. She ambled over in seemingly weightless steps to the lectern and nudged it an inch. She looked over the sanctuary. *Father is due back from the Baptist conference in Gauhati today. My new hymn is finished. I have rehearsed it in secret so he will be the first to hear it. Many people, even Hindus and Muslims, come to our services only to hear me sing.* Mara closed her eyes, steepled her hands, and looked to the sky. "Heavenly Father, in the name of Jesus, may the Holy Spirit use my hymn to touch hearts with Jesus's love and deliverance."

Mara took a final glance at the sanctuary and waited outside on the veranda. School was not in session, and the clinic was calm. She reached into her pocket and pulled out her handwritten hymn. After perusing it, she tweaked a lyric and a note. Her father had taught her English and her mother Assamese from before she could remember. Her mother taught her to read and write music, play the piano, and coached her voice using their old Broadwood and Sons upright piano.

She hummed the tune of her new hymn to herself while gazing down Sundarpur's main road. Common survival knowledge among her compatriots was that cobras and vipers have no ears but can feel vibrations. Mara sensed imperceptible vibrations in the hard-packed earthen road that the oxen-led bullock cart bringing her father home drew near. The first sound was the clinking of oxen's bells; next came hooves clanking on the road and clucking chickens scurrying aside. She spotted the tall missionary sitting stiff-backed on the hard seat. Gray dust powdered his long black coat, matching his short hair and trimmed beard. Her heart lifted. Mara ran to the center of the road, smiled, and waved. He beamed and waved back. The carter disembarked from his front plank and assisted Mara's father from the cart. Afterwards, the carter stacked the Reverend's two bags and a package next to him.

"Father!" Mara embraced him. "My prayers were answered. You're home safe."

"And my prayers, too. You look as beautiful as ever, my wonderful daughter. Next time, I will take you with me. You're a woman now and deserve another trip to Guahati. I want you to experience the colors and hustle and bustle of the markets on your own. It will further enrich you. The Bible requires modesty and decorum. It never says a woman can't look beautiful. God asks that we use our talents to his glory. India has many gods. Your voice and beauty draw people to our church. It opens the door for us to plant the seed of our Lord and Savior, Jesus Christ, the only way to the one true Father. A beautiful sight will enhance your beautiful sound. I decided to do my part. The other day, I got a break from the conference and did some shopping in Gauhati's markets. Here's what I found for you." He handed her a two-foot-long, light, rectangular box.

"I think it's a…" Mara beamed and pulled the top off the box. "Huh!" She held the lavender blue dress in front of her. The cotton fabric seemed to smile with the sunlight. Narrow pintucks were stitched across the bodice while a simple white sash added a touch of freshness. "It's gorgeous, Father! I love it! Thank you!"

"Well, that's not all. Good things often come in small packages." From his coat pocket, he drew a small, round case of polished silver not much larger than a pocket watch.

Mara's mouth opened to form a near-perfect circle. "Huh." She covered her mouth with her palms. Her father took her hand and placed the item in her palm. The item's hinge clicked as she opened it. Inside lay a little round mirror that reflected the Assam sunlight, and beneath it a wafer of pale powder with a downy puff the size of an American silver dollar. She looked up at her father with doe-like eyes. She wanted to speak, but her vocal cords froze as if she were asleep in a dream.

"And these will make you feel clean and fresh." Brian Sutcliffe handed his daughter a small, white cardboard box with four bars of scented soap. "You're a woman now, and a strong Christian woman at that. Therefore, I have something else for you." He reached into his satchel and handed her a parcel wrapped in a linen handkerchief, tied with a ribbon.

Mara hesitated before taking it.

Her father nodded.

She untied the ribbon and removed the item from the handkerchief. "Huh! Father! I don't know what to say." Mara stared at the curved tortoise shell comb before running it through her midnight black hair. "This is the happiest day of my life!"

"This is the day that I will look at you as a woman rather than a little girl. I could not be prouder of you. The village is grateful for what you do as a teacher and a nurse. You are a blessing to everyone you encounter. I have given almost my entire adult life to our Lord Jesus. A daughter like you is a greater reward than anything I could ever deserve." Reverend Sutcliffe placed his hand on Mara's arm. "Let's go inside. I can't wait to see your mother, and I'm half starved."

***

Leena Sutcliffe greeted her husband with a warm smile and a gentle embrace. She met her American husband while a Music major at Bethane College in Calcutta. She taught Mara how to read sheet music. Along with her husband, they taught Mara the nuances of the Italian, French, and German languages. Slender as opposed to her husband's sturdy frame and standing shorter than her daughter, her smooth skin glowed like rich caramel. She wore a traditional two-piece sari that loosely draped her body. Her eyes shifted to the parcels in her daughter's arms, erasing her smile.

She tightened her lips and sat at their dining table. "I helped Jolani," Leena nodded at their female house servant, "prepare us a meal of warm curried lamb. I knew your journey would leave you in hunger."

"Father, I finished writing my new hymn. I waited for you to come home before I shared it with anyone."

Lena ate a forkful of curried lamb. "Why not surprise us this Sunday at church?"

Brian smiled at his wife.

Leena did not return his smile.

"That sounds like a great idea, Leena." Brian folded his hands. "I am certain you will make us even prouder parents this Sunday morning."

"If you will excuse me," Mara wiped her lip with a linen napkin and stood, "I am going to practice it in the sanctuary." She chuckled. "Don't sneak in and spoil your surprise."

After Mara left the room and closed the door behind her, Leena held her husband's hand and looked at him in solemn calm. "I know you want to make our daughter happy. I also know that I am having trouble seeing her as a grown woman, but she will always be my little girl. We sent Christopher to Boston for a better education and opportunity. But he's a young man and can deal with the perils of an American city. Still, seeing him off was the saddest day of my life, and I miss him terribly, and Mara misses her brother as well. I could never bear saying goodbye to my daughter, and the village would be at a terrible loss without her. She teaches at our school, serves at the clinic, and especially wins souls for Jesus by singing in the church. Her natural beauty is not escaping notice. But are powders, mirrors, and colorful clothes right for her? Will it distract her from the Lord's work? Worse, will enriching her outer beauty draw eyes she does not need?"

"Leena, it is no sin for Mara to see herself as the Lord made her. I want her to know she is lovely in his sight."

"I only wish for her to be safe. The world does not guard its eyes, and you know that men not of our faith attend our church only to see her. Modesty, as Apostle Paul teaches, is her shield."

"Confidence can only make her a better servant of the Lord. We taught her that she is God's daughter, and she has always walked upright. A colorful dress and a comb for her hair will not change that."

"I have faith in Mara as my daughter and you as my husband. I only pray that she keeps her heart set on Christ, not on adornments."

"As I also do, Leena. I have faith that Mara will know she can be both devout and beautiful. The two are not enemies. Besides, we have prayed that in his good timing, God will send her a worthy husband, and we'll have grandchildren to raise to God's glory." Brian took Leena's hand. They touched foreheads and prayed together.

***

Sunday morning. Corporal Stanton and Lawrence Mills sipped tea on the Dak veranda. "You'd best hurry up and finish, mate." Douglas Stanton took a final sip from his cup and placed it on the saucer. "I can see from here that people are already milling around the church. We'd better go now if you want to see the woman behind the voice."

Lawrence put his cup on the saucer without finishing, wiped his mouth with a linen cloth, and stood. "You're right. As you would say to your troops, 'Forward March.'"

***

Throngs of villagers from every socio-economic standing, and a few British soldiers and railway officials, wedged their way into the church for the morning English service. The Assamese language service would not be held until the afternoon. Nevertheless, Lawrence and Douglas could hear the name Mara above the Assamese chatter. Douglas pulled his rifle from his shoulder and held it at port arms. "Move aside!" The crowd parted.

"Don't." Lawrence grabbed his arm. "I'm not much of a believer, but let's respect the people and this church as a house of God; we'll take our places with everyone else." Douglas tensed his lips and narrowed his eyes before complying. They entered the church with the others and stood together at the rear.

***

Reverend Sutcliffe stood behind the lectern and raised his arms to preach the final words of his sermon. "My friends, with great honor and love, I told you the truth and the good news. Your soul's salvation is free to you, but at a terrible cost to the Lord. Salvation is not found in multiple gods, nor in idols crafted by man, nor in the dreams of mortal prophets who lie dead in their tombs. Only the Son rose from the dead and left an empty tomb. For there is but one God who created the heavens and earth, one Father who loves you so much that he sacrificed his Son for you, one Savior who died, and one Savior who rose from the dead, ascended into Heaven, and will come again. All other lights are but shadows- only one is the true light that shines in the darkness. You may seek truth in many places, but truth has only one name: Jesus Christ. In him is life, both now and forevermore. Amen. I appreciate your attendance and respect. Thank you for letting me share the true gospel of Jesus Christ. He is a God of freedom. He gives you the choice to receive him into your heart or to reject him. It's no secret why many of you are here. That moment has arrived. My daughter Mara has composed a new hymn. May the beauty of her voice bring the word of our Lord into your hearts."

Mara walked across the front of the church as gracefully as if the floor were a cloud. She wore her new lavender blue gown, and a touch of powder gave her cheeks a ruby glow. Her long, dark tresses were brushed out and adorned with a jasmine flower. She had tossed her hair over her right shoulder. She stood before the lectern and faced the congregation. Only the faint song of a distant jungle bird broke the silence. She nodded to her mother, who sat behind their Broadwood and Sons upright piano and played the opening notes. Mara sang,

"You only live once, on this earthly shore,
Your soul is a treasure, worth so much more.
Though sorrows may stay, and years drift away,
One Savior has come to show you the way."

"One life, then eternity,
The cross has won our victory.
Rejoice, he has paid the price,
No second death, but eternal life."

"He calls the lost, through the darkest night,
His mercy is strong; his love shines bright.
The gate is narrow, but the shepherd will guide,
His word shows the way; his arms open wide."

"One life, then eternity,
The cross has won our victory.
Rejoice, he has paid the price,
No second death, but eternal life."

"When shadows falter, and dawn appears,
He'll banish all pain and dry all our tears.
A crown of life he will give to all who believe,
and life without end, his children receive."

"One life, then eternity,
The cross has won our victory.
All praise to the risen Son,
The Lamb, our only One."

The congregation sat breathless, unsure of whether to applaud or to remain silent. Lawrence made eye contact with Mara. She smiled and blushed before lowering her head and slinking away. After Mara vanished, the congregation clapped and cheered, many shouting praises to the Lord.

"She smiled at you, mate!" Douglas punched Lawrence's arm. "I've never heard of her smiling at a man that way. If she can't make you forget Dorothy, then you're suffering from an incurable strain of jungle fever, my lad." Lawrence stood still, staring at the spot where Mara exited the sanctuary.

Chapter 6

Lawrence sat on his horse. He checked his map before looking over scores of workers, oxen, and two elephants. The jungle seemed to sing to him. Tree branches rustled in the breeze; sunlight gleamed a rainbow of colors from the shiny emerald leaves and fronds. He closed his eyes. The warmth of the morning sun evoked an image of Mara. *Mara, Mara, your skin looked so soft and smooth, your hair so dark and luxuriant, and that precious, fleeting second of gazing into your big brown eyes. Yet your voice, your voice, is the music of your voice breaking Dorothy's torment? Is the God you sang of the spirit I lack? Or did someone cast an unholy spell?* Lawrence noticed vivid clusters of scarlet, pink, and deep red rhododendron blossoms and bright orange jungle geraniums dancing among the jungle's dominant emerald. He walked over and picked a bright crimson Hibiscus flower. *He brushed the petals with his nose, savoring the aroma before placing the flower into Mara's hair...*A violent rustling gave way to a sharp crack; the fallen tree hit the ground with a harsh thud, breaking Lawrence's funk. The workers dispersed while yelling a jumble of Assamese words and phrases. The huge banyan tree almost crushed them. It lay across the path that took days of work to clear. The workers looked like feckless mice trying to redirect the startled elephants and oxen. The four British soldiers circled them.

"Halt!" Lawrence yelled in Assamese. "Halt!" The Sirdar ran up to Lawrence and awaited instructions. "Tell them to leave the tree for now. We need to clear the bank. The bridge team will make a retaining wall, then we'll add fill." Lawrence perused his paperwork. He motioned to a worker. He sprinted over with his surveying equipment. The Sirdar set up his theodolite. Lawrence spoke while looking through the scope. "We will need at least a five-degree turn here. It will require an extra seven chains of track, but it will be well worth it. The trains will not be forced to slow down. That's all, Sirdar."

The Sirdar blasted his buffalo Pepa horn before shouting to the workers in Assamese. They went to work clearing the bank.

A reed-thin, barefoot man ran up to Corporal Stanton and handed him a half-inch thick, eight-inch-long cylinder. The corporal opened the cylinder and removed the message. The messenger slightly bowed with his palms pressed together. The Corporal handed back the cylinder and dismissed him. He ran off in the direction from which he came.

Corporal Stanton rode his horse over to Lawrence. "Mr. Mills, mate, you're the only one here who didn't react to the falling Banyon tree." He smirked at Lawrence. "I think I know why. One might ask why a bird you never truly met has you so smitten. Ahh," Corporal Stanton raised his palms. "But in the case of a peach like Mara, I ain't say I blame ya." He grinned.

"You're right." Lawrence blushed. "A lady landed me here in the first place. Mara sang about life after death. I'd better be more alert. You're right, Douglas. I wasn't paying attention because I was daydreaming about her. I guess that's a damn sight better than pining for the woman I lost." Lawrence pursed his lips and shook his head. "That tree could've made me find out if Mara was right about life after death. Her song hypnotized me. It hypnotized me beyond experiencing Wagner's Ring at New York's Metropolitan Opera House.

"Well, mate, I admit, I've heard talk about Wagner's Ring, but I can't say I've ever got to hear a performance. But, Mara, her song hypnotized me just the same." Douglas shook his head. "The Crown frowns upon me romancing locals, and I'm a soldier first. Lucky you, mate." He laughed. "Mara makes me wish I were a Yank. In the meantime, here's a message for you."

Lawrence took the message from the corporal and read it. *Report to Sir Nigel Browning at his estate at noon tomorrow.* The note was signed, Fredrick Robert Upcott, Railway Board Chairman.

Chapter 7

Lawrence told the Sirdar to break the workforce for lunch. After the Sirdar blasted his Pepa buffalo horn, Lawrence took a final look at the work site before riding his horse to Sir Nigel Browning's tea plantation. Within two hours, he arrived at the privately cleared spur to Sir Nigel Browning's manor. *The grade is too steep for steam locomotives and freight cars. It will require considerably more grading. It will not come cheaply.* He rode his horse in a slow four-beat gait past the newly constructed warehouse and processing plant. *'It's cleared for a triple track siding. He'll have to pay extra for the third track. Current policy allows only one siding track per structure.* Lawrence noticed that the tea plantation laborers did not stop working to look at him. Lawrence rode along a hard-packed earth and gravel drive. *Am I still in India? Sir Nigel's manor house is impressive. If not for this blasted heat and tropical flora, it would remind me of the Cabot Estate mansion outside of Wayne, Pennsylvania, only this one is grander. I'd best deal with Sir Nigel accordingly.*

A stocky man, wearing a black salwar and achkan, topped by a white turban that added several inches to his already intimidating height, and armed with a curved Tulwar sword, greeted Lawrence. "Mr. Browning will see you inside." Lawrence dismounted. Browning's bodyguard and bearer secured Lawrence's horse before showing him into the house.

Nigel Browning stood tall, posture carved in stone. He looked down, his eyes sharp and unblinking, making Lawrence's nerves jitter. "Welcome, Mr. Mills."

Each measured syllable of Sir. Browning's deep, baritone voice sent a tremor through Lawrence's nerves. *He's far more formidable than George Cabot,* Lawrence thought as he swallowed back saliva.

Sir Nigel extended his hand. He gripped Lawrence's hand a shade stronger and held it a beat longer. "Follow me to my drawing room. My maid servants will bring us refreshments. We have much to discuss, Mr. Mills."

Sir Nigel walked a step ahead of Lawrence, making him think the glass eyes of Sir Nigel's tiger, leopard, and horned antelope trophies were watching him. Lawrence fell another step behind his host to admire the formal, oil-painted portraits of Browning ancestors, fox-hunting and equestrian scenes, landscapes of the English countryside, and exotic portrayals of India, all mounted in gilded frames.

A Gueridon stand held a vase from the Ming Dynasty, and a console table against the wall displayed Japanese Inari plates. Lawrence entered the Browning drawing room and glanced at his reflection in one of two huge gilt-framed mirrors. He straightened his posture to match the nearly half foot that Sir Nigel had on him.

"Sit." Nigel opened his hand and motioned to a high-backed chair. Lawrence sat while Sir Nigel remained standing and saying nothing.

"I am certain," Lawrence cleared his throat and swallowed saliva, "you wish to discuss our building a railway spur to your new commercial buildings."

"We will get to that. First, I want to meet the man that Fredrick Robert Upcott made Engineer in Charge. We should share a gin and tonic. It's far better to get to know a man over a drink." Sir Nigel snapped his fingers. The jingle of ankle bells preceded the two female servants' entrance to the drawing room.

Lawrence momentarily ceased to focus on his host. *They're stunning. Dorothy was beautiful but not unique. I've never seen anything like these two in America or Europe, except for Mara. Mara...Why do you so suddenly haunt me?*

"I see that Anjali and Layla please you." Nigel broke Lawrence's reverie. "India has many treasures. You will agree that beautiful women are far greater treasures than any amount of tea, or gold and gemstones for that matter."

Lawrence's mind remained blank; his vocal cords froze.

Layla and Anjali wore midnight black silk saris that caught the lamplight in waves of silver and indigo. They were pleated low across their hips, clinging with near liquid intimacy to their curves. The Pallu, the long end, was cast over each of their shoulders, sheer enough to hint at the form beneath. Thick and glossy raven hair enhanced their oval faces. Their lustrous skin shone like polished amber. *Their dark almond-like eyes are shapely enough and set to a sculptor's norm.* Lawrence pinched his chin. *But they remind me too much of the glass eyes of Sir Nigel's hunting trophies.*

Both Anjali and Layla carried silver trays. Anjali placed her tray on the table. Lawrence fixed his eyes on them. *Such long and beautifully toned arms. Their every movement seems like measured feminine grace.* Layla took two long-stem, crystal goblets from the tray and placed them in front of Lawrence and Nigel. Layla put ice cubes into their glasses before grasping the decanter by the handle and pouring its contents into their glasses. Anjali topped off their glasses with liquid from a smaller container.

"Ahh," Nigel at last smiled at Lawrence. "Tonic for fever and gin for courage, with ice cubes rarer than both." Lawrence snapped his fingers. Anjali and Layla, without turning their backs, retreated seven paces, their ankle bells jingling. They stood upright, hands folded at their waists, and their eyes cast downward. He next raised his glass. "To a profitable friendship." Lawrence and Nigel touched glasses. "Drink." Nigel waited for Lawrence to sip first, ensuring that he drank more than he did. "At last, I meet the man whom George Cabot spoke so highly of."

Lawrence almost dropped his glass. "George Cabot! Do you know George Cabot? What did he say about me? Did he say anything about his daughter, Dorothy?"

Sir Nigel held up his hand. "America still trails the Old Country in culture and refinement, but you're gaining on us in wealth. A man in George Cabot's position would not risk his personal and business reputation by recommending anyone less than the best for the Assam Bengal Railway. I hear in your voice that you fancy his daughter. Succeed for me, and I can exert my influence on Mr. Cabot's opinion of you. That's assuming you don't find something better in Raj India." Nigel motioned his head toward Anjali and Layla.

Lawrence took a furtive glance at Sir Nigel's maidservants. "I will, of course, conduct a thorough survey of your path. I commend you for taking initiative, and I'm sure it's proven sufficient for a horse-drawn carriage. Nevertheless, before we can even think of laying rails for a steam locomotive, it will need extensive grading, including cuts, fills, retaining walls, and at least two small bridges. The cost will prove substantial."

Sir Nigel remained quiet and still.

Lawrence cleared his throat. "Another issue is that it appears from your construction that you will require a third siding. Current policy is one siding per structure. You must pay for the third siding. It's also policy that construction on the spur will not commence until the main line to the port of Chittagong is completed."

"The crown has decided to pay for the spur to my plantation." Sir Nigel sipped his gin and tonic. "For good reason. We both know that the line will move coal, timber, and oil. Nevertheless, the railway will not turn a profit without tea plantations such as mine. We both know that you're not working on behalf of the natives, but for my gain and for the Crown to both make money and strengthen its grip on its colony." He placed his glass on the table and snapped his fingers. Layla and Anjali strode over and filled their glasses. Their lilac aroma mingled with the lime flavor of their drinks. "You are building the line to serve interests such as mine. I can't see you holding up the project by demanding that I contribute to its construction." Sir Nigel nodded to Lawrence and motioned with his right hand at his drink.

"I am an engineer, not a chairman. I don't set policy. I only supervise the construction of the railway's path." Lawrence tensed his lips, picked up his glass, but returned it to the table without drinking.

"Ahh, yes, even though you're a Yankee civilian, I do see that you have the discipline and courage that won your country's independence. We fought again in 1812, but we won't fight here. Perhaps this will settle the matter." Sir Nigel snapped his fingers twice. His huge turbaned bodyguard walked over. He glared at Lawrence before handing him a document.

Lawrence's jaw dropped as he read, *I hereby authorize and order you to spare no expense in clearing the spur to Sir Nigel's plantation. Construction is to commence immediately. All work, to include the sidings at Sir Nigel's production plant, will be borne at the expense of the King and the Assam-Bengal Railway. Ensure that it meets or exceeds the King's highest standards so that it may earn both profit and control for the empire.* Frederick Robert Upcott had signed the document. It included his official stamp as Chairman of the Railway Board. Lawrence placed the document on the table.

Sir Nigel held eye contact, a heartbeat long enough for Lawrence to look away. Browning pressed his lips into a thin line and tilted his head slightly. "Now that you know Chairman Upcott has authorized everything that I need, you may relax and enjoy your drink. Let's discuss the real reason I summoned you."

The ice cubes of Lawrence's drink rattled against his glass as he lifted it to his lips.

"I have more reach in the colony and beyond than you may realize. My sources tell me many things about you. All of them are good, but I wanted to find out for myself." Sir Nigel steepled his hands with fingers and thumbs touching. "Tell me, Mr. Mills, what is your religion?"

"I prefer to judge a man by his honor, rather than his creed. I strive to be a man of conscience, sir."

Sir Nigel remained silent. He thickened the silence with a heavy stare.

Lawrence broke the silence. He could hear his voice in a fuzzy hush. "If you must know, sir, I was raised a Presbyterian, and, to answer your question truthfully and directly, I remain unsure."

"I would expect nothing less than absolute honesty from you, Mr. Mills, for I do believe, as you so eloquently stated, that you are a man of honor." Sir Nigel placed his palms flat on the table. "Do not all Western faiths worship one supreme being? Does not one high-ranking religionist decide what you are to believe and how you are to interpret their Scriptures?"

"Before I came to India, I would have wholly agreed with you." Lawrence opened his hands. "But just recently, I learned from an American service held in Sundarpur, what I was missing after years of church back home. The Christian God loves us, and he sent his son Jesus to suffer death as payment for our sins. While all other prophets remained in their grave, Jesus rose from the dead."

"Bravo." Nigel mockingly clapped his hands. "Well recited. Don't think for a second that I am unaware of what Christian missions preach. Their message is predictable, as you have just proven. Now tell me." He touched his fingers and thumbs. "What do you truly believe?"

"I am an engineer, Sir Nigel, not a theologian or philosopher, so I am sure it would be of little interest to a man of your schooling and intellect."

"My schooling? A true higher education dictates that an intellectual considers every source." Sir Nigel opened his hands.

"Seeing how you put it, yes, it makes sense to me on an intellectual level." Lawrence forced Anjali and Layla from his thoughts and pictured Mara, replaying her hymn in his mind. "It took a most enchanting woman with a mesmerizing voice to make me consider it at a deeper, spiritual level."

"A woman?" Nigel smirked at him. He snapped his finger. Layla and Anjali strode over to him. Each placed a hand on his shoulder. Anjali let her hand slide to his pectorals. Layla moved behind him and massaged his shoulders. "When you learn that we are to possess mortal women and not let them possess us, you may reach your potential. Your infatuation with Dorothy Cabot played a role in bringing you to me." Nigel glanced at his maidservants. They snuggled closer to him. "That's the last time such weakness will be to your benefit."

Lawrence couldn't help but imbibe their lilac scent. He licked his lips, closed his eyes, and breathed deeply.

"Do my maidservants evoke what religionists call sinful thoughts, Mr. Mills? What if I were to loan them to you? Would it be a sin? After all, what is sin?"

Lawrence glanced at Layla and Anjali and squeezed the lion's head at the end of the armchair. He looked away and faced Sir Nigel. "I would say sin is disobedience to God."

"I would say that's nonsense and that true sin is denying yourself the riches that this world has to offer. Did not Oscar Wilde first publish in your hometown of Philadelphia's *Lippincott's Monthly Magazine, A Picture of Dorian Gray?*

"Yes, Sir Nigel, I read it."

"Do you not remember the passage as spoken by Lord Henry Wotton, 'The best way to get rid of temptation is to yield to it, as temptation is not temptation at all but opportunity, and if you pass on an opportunity, you will regret it in the future'." Sir Nigel paused, waiting for Lawrence's reaction before continuing. "If I were to avail you of Layla or Anaji, and you were to refuse, would that not be an opportunity that you would regret in the future?

Lawrence looked away from Anaji and Layla. "Of course, I find them attractive. I'm a man, aren't I? Just what is your game, sir?" He extended his open right hand. "You already got what you want from the Railroad Chairman. My job is to build the main line, and now it includes your spur. I am committed to doing my job and doing it well."

Nigel Browning grinned and tilted his head slightly to his right. "I detect from your vocal tone that I made you think. I have summoned many to my drawing room." He held his steepled hands with fingers and thumbs touching in front of his chest, "including high-ranking local authorities, British military officers, and British civilian officials, such as the Chairman of the Railway Board, Frederick Robert Upcott. He is no different than you or the others. All have looked upon Layla and Anjali with lust and desire. You told me that your church in America taught you Bible scriptures. Correct?"

Lawrence nodded.

Sir Nigel folded his hands behind his head. So, tell me, Mr. Mills, when Satan tempted Jesus with all the world's kingdoms, would it have been true temptation if he could not make good on his offer? Out of my many visitors, Mr. Lawrence Mills, you are among the few that I have offered the pleasure of my maidservants."

Lawrence sat silently. His eyes blinked rapidly.

Nigel paused for effect, "That's because it's you whom I find most promising." Nigel Browning stood. "Come with me. I wish to show you something I have shown no outsider."

***

Sir Nigel ushered Lawrence toward one of the manor's rear doors. The clanging of a heavy latch punctuated Nigel's opening of it. Sir Nigel stood aside for Lawrence to exit first. He tipped his wide-brimmed felt hat to shield his eyes from the noon sun.

Ahead, set apart from the manor, rose a structure that Lawrence had not noticed from the road. Its walls gleamed in the sun; its roofline drawn high and narrow like a spire, every corner sharp against the sky. A spiked wrought iron fence enclosed its grounds. Sir Nigel opened the broad gate and motioned for Lawrence to enter. He walked in a wide path among Serpents coiled at a god's feet and a purple goddess sitting astride a tiger, both arranged like attendants in a court. *These appear as lesser lights. Why do I suspect that Browning has something up his sleeve?*

Sir Nigel opened the building's hardwood and riveted bronze door. "Welcome to my sanctuary, Mr. Mills."

Lawrence gazed at the shadows cast upon pillars and carved symbols. *What are they?* Lawrence touched his chin. *The chancel. Why is it empty?*

"You are honored among men to gain admittance to my sanctum. I decide if you will be honored among the gods."

"Gods? Is that God in the plural?"

"Where are you now, Mr. Mills?"

"I know I am in British Raj India. Where I am at this moment leaves me at a loss."

"Dorothy left you, Mr. Mills. Yet you still pine for her."

Lawrence turned pale; his jaw dropped.

"Unlike your former fiancé, my wife, Theresa, followed me here. Perhaps I was mistaken in bringing her. She passed while giving birth to my son. He was stillborn, Mr. Mills. Did our so-called one almighty God intervene? How far away is his so-called Heaven?"

"How can anyone know?" Lawrence spread his palms.

"Good answer, Mr. Mills." Sir Nigel tensed his lips. "Why worship a distant, indifferent God, when you can be a god? Why worship an unseen deity when you can be the object of worship? What if you could wield godlike power? Why let a woman possess your heart, only to let outside forces, whether a disapproving family or an angry God, crush it like an insect?"

"What about Anaji and Layla?" Lawrence wiped sweat from his brow with his hand. "They are beautiful. They are exotic in a way no Western woman can ever be."

"Again, I state, Mr. Mills, we are to possess women. They must never possess us. Comely as we both find Anjali and Layla, I can replace them at my whim. Don't you want that power? To have beautiful women at your beck and call, as well as have both the poor and rich joyfully hand over their wealth to you?"

"Why do you need money from the poor? Your tea plantation and your family's wealth are more than any man could ever need."

"I might say that you disappoint me, Mr. Mills." Sir Nigel's lips curled slightly upward. "But I know that you will prove to be a fast learner. This is not just about money, and it's surely not about need. There are many Gods, Mr. Mills, and not all are living in a distant, unknown realm of the universe. A similarity that the Protestants, Catholics, and even the Jews and Muslims share is a belief in one supreme, divine being. They are blind to the many gods. Kali is the highest and ultimate God, or better, shall I say, Goddess."

Sir Nigel led Lawrence to the empty chancel. "You may have noticed that my chancel is empty. Have you noted its cleanliness? It awaits Kali's purity. The blood of the universe courses through her veins. She is both the creator and the destroyer. Destruction, Mr. Mills, is the world's sole comfort. I know what the bishops and ministers, the imams and rabbis, don't. Destruction is the world's only comfort, and renewal is its highest gift. Death and birth are the same breath drawn twice. Kali is time itself.

She ends the ages so that the wheel may turn again. Her dance is not cruelty, it's mercy. Imagine a surgeon cutting away gangrene. So, she does for the world. This chancel awaits her. I have yet to find an artist or sculptor who is equal to the task of capturing her beauty in image or statue. When that Kali arrives, I shall become the mighty god Shiva and dance with her. Kali is eternal and immortal. Our dance will unite as one in immortality and power. A billion Hindus will worship us. The Christians, Muslims, and Jews will question their beliefs and soon fall to their knees before us."

"In all due respect, Sir Nigel, you're insane."

"You have great courage, Mr. Mills. I can have you disappear without a trace, and no one would be the wiser." Sir Nigel placed his hands on Lawrence's shoulders. "Consider all I have shown you. The wealth of my plantation and family. The beauty and desirability of my maidservants. My dominance over your chairman. You heard me correctly; I control the man who signs your paychecks and whose word can make or break your career. Yet Robert Fredrick Upcott cowered at my presence. I considered him for what I am offering you, but he proved weak and corrupt."

Sir Nigel stood straighter, narrowed and sharpened his gaze into Lawrence's eyes, all while cracking a smile. "You dared to look me in the eye and question my sanity. Now that you know I am sound, I will dub you Skanda. Kali will adopt you as her son. When the mother returns, her son must prepare the way.

Just as you now prepare the railroad for a mighty empire, you will be as a general, leading Kali's soldiers in the destruction that brings renewal. As the son of a goddess, you may choose your partner. Once I dance with Kali and she empowers me as Shiva, we can return Dorothy to you. Or, if you wish to remain single, you can have access to concubines as lovely as Anjali and Layla.

Although you will remain subordinate to me and Kali, your power, wealth, and splendor will exceed that of the most privileged mortal man.

Even George Cabot will drop to his knees and bow before your presence. Before you answer, Mr. Mills, why not experience the adventure of the land you will help me and Kali rule? In two days, I am embarking on a tiger hunt. Join me, Mr. Mills."

Chapter 8

The rising midday sun signaled the end of another school day. Mara pinched her grandmother's silver crucifix, smiled at it, and stood before the children. She wore her white dress but had brightened her cheeks with a pinch of powder. "Class, before I dismiss you for the day. I want to sing you a song. Listen to the first verse, then join me in the refrain.

The class applauded and cheered.

Mara sang,

"Jesus loves the little ones,

Morning, noon, and night.

When we pray, he hears our voice,

Always shining on us his holy light."

Mara spoke, "Now sing along." She waved her hands like an orchestra conductor with a baton. The class sang with her.

"We walk in his love,

We walk in his care;

Wherever we go,

Our savior is there."

Mara spotted her father smiling at her in the doorway. She returned his smile before turning back to her class. "Class dismissed."

While the class started filing toward the door, a little girl asked, "Is there any homework?"

"Hold up, class." Mara walked over to the door and blocked the pupils from leaving. "Your homework is to read in your New

Testament, Mathew 5, 14, 16, and write a paragraph about what it means to you."

"Thanks a lot, Padma." A young boy lightly punched her arm.

"Just for that, Arum," Mara stepped in between them. "You get to write two paragraphs."

Brian Sutcliffe walked over to his daughter. "God has blessed you with many gifts. Not the least of which is your ability to relate and communicate with children. I am prouder of you than a man is permitted. But your humility makes my pride acceptable."

"Thank you, father," Mara blushed and lowered her head.

"And your mother." Brian touched his daughter's hand. "She doesn't express it in words as I do; nevertheless, she taught you music, both piano and voice. Unfortunately, your brother never took to music. But you? Your mother's expression when she hears you sing says more than any number of words. Mara, we both know that you haven't sung for anyone outside of Sundarpur. The children in our school adore hearing you, and your voice even helps to heal patients in the clinic. At the very least, it relieves their pain. We seldom have access to doctors or medicine. Praise the Lord," Reverend Sutcliffe raised his hands, "your singing to them is more important than you realize."

"Thank you, father. I know God has given me a gift. But how can I spread it far and wide without taking from others? Sundarpur's children need our school, and where would the village be without the clinic?"

"Mara, your voice and the new hymn you sang last Sunday have sown the wind and reaped the whirlwind. News of your voice has spread far and wide via the bazaar telegraph. Your voice is no longer a lamplight hidden under a bed. I just received an actual telegraph from Gauhati. It comes from Bishop Fregosi from St. Joseph's Cathedral. He wants you to sing at their Friday night service."

"Huh," Mara covered her face. "The St. Joseph's Cathedral is huge, Father." She lowered her gaze and wrung her hands. "I have only sung in our little schoolhouse and chapel. In the schoolhouse, the bright eyes of the children carry me on. In our chapel, Mother playing the piano for me pads my confidence. But to sing for over a thousand people? And to a huge organ played by a stranger? I don't know if I am ready, Father."

"We are Baptists and under no obligation to even a Bishop or the Pope, for that matter. On the other hand, a leader as important as a Bishop asking a Protestant to sing at his Cathedral and to his flock should tell you how great an impression you made. Moreover, he doesn't want you to change so much as one word of your hymn. Your voice and your gift of songwriting will bolster the faith of Christian believers of all denominations and bring unbelievers to saving faith." Reverend Sutcliffe squeezed his daughter's hand. "If God be for us, who can be against us?"

"Will you accompany me, Father?"

"Of course, Mara. And your mother, too. When two or more are gathered in his name, the Lord will be present. We will stay in prayer. You will prove a great blessing to many. And, seeing that you're going to sing in a grand cathedral and in front of well over a thousand people, on this even your mother will agree, a trip to the Gauhati market for a beautiful new dress is in order."

Mara beamed.

Chapter 9

Lawrence rode his horse on the improved spur to Sir Nigel's plantation. Stacked in geometric precision and blackened with thick coats of creosote, the railway ties resembled a string of cuboid boxes. Their tar-laden scent mingled with the jungle's morning mist. Next to it, piles of steel rails reflected the rising sun with flashes of blue and red.

He dismounted to inspect a new retaining wall and fill. *This curve is a degree sharper than I would like. It will prove sufficient for an industrial spur, however.* He rode a mile farther. *The bridge team constructed this quickly.* Lawrence pinched his chin. *I see no sign of hasty workmanship. It should pass inspection and be deemed ready for rails. When that happens, I will probably earn a bonus. I'll ask the Railway Board to award the men who did the real work.* Lawrence tipped his felt-brimmed hat. *The British government paid for all of this. I'll ask Browning to share a fraction of his gain with the men who sweated and toiled. Christian, Muslim, and Jewish sects all give to the poor. Even George Cabot established charity foundations. Diana Cabot, with Dorothy's help,* Lawrence pinched his eyelids shut, *worked tirelessly for the community. Maybe I'll see merit in Sir Nigel's belief in Kali, or at least his version of the Hindu goddess, if he would do likewise.* Lawrence rode the final stretch to the Browning estate. *The graders will have to redo this portion. Without looking through my theodolite, I can tell this grade is a half percentage too steep.*

Lawrence first heard elephants trumpeting and a cacophony of shouting voices in Assamese. He reached a clearing and saw a half dozen elephants lined up in a semicircle. Their gray hides were streaked with dust and battle scars, while their tusks were filed smooth and polished. Even from a distance, Lawrence detected a fury in them unlike the railway crew's *kumkis* working elephants. Mahouts were perched on their necks, poised and still like crocodiles waiting in ambush. Forty Assamese beaters, armed only with sticks, awaited on foot.

Sir Nigel stood beside an elephant wearing an elaborate howdah enhanced with high-relief work of colorful indigenous artistry depicting tigers and elephants. He was clad in a light khaki drill jacket, tailored close and worn stiff on his shoulders. Its brass buttons were polished to a glow. Cut from cream twill, his trousers were tucked into shiny, blackened leather boots. He tipped his pith helmet on spotting Lawrence. Nigel stood still and straight, hands at his side.

Larence instinctively hastened his gait and walked up to him.

"I'm pleased that you arrived on time. You will ride with me. As you can see, my Kumeriah elephants are of the highest breed. All military, professional, and social ranks are cast aside during the hunt. I am in charge. You may have noticed Railway Chairman Upcott." Nigel pointed to another elephant. "In that elephant is Colonel Hutchins of the Royal Army, commander of the Assamese regiment, and there is Prince Alaric of Schwatzenheim. Today, you outrank them all. Consider this your dress rehearsal for the power and prestige that awaits you when Kali adopts you as her son, Skanda. And speaking of dress, this is the last time you go on a tiger hunt wearing your work clothes. If you're going to ride with me as second in command, and if I'm going to promote you over men of higher social and professional standing, I need you to look the part." Browning turned and nodded to the Mahout.

At the Mahout's cry, the elephant sank to its knees. Sir Nigel mounted first. He climbed up the rope ladder, grabbed the curved rail of the howdah, and swung his tall frame into place as easily as mounting his horse. After settling into his seat, he nodded at Lawrence. He took a running start and grabbed the rope ladder. It swayed in his grip. "Damn," Browning muttered as his boot hit the elephant's side and slipped from the ladder's rung. Lawrence held on by squeezing the ladder's rails hard enough to make his knuckles turn white. Browning's derisive laughter laced Lawrence's embarrassment. He managed to get his boot back into the rung and climb upward. Sir Nigel reached out, grabbed Lawrence's wrist, and pulled him into the howdah like a fisherman dragging his thrashing tuna over a boat's gunwale. Lawrence noticed that even the beaters were sniggering.

"Welcome aboard, Mr. Mills. This will be your rifle." Nigel pointed at a Winchester .405 bolt-action rifle. "As the lead hunter, I will use this .500 NE Westley Richards double-barreled. Our goal is to kill the tiger with one shot. Let's hope the extra barrel or backup weapon will prove unnecessary." Sir Nigel snapped his fingers. The Mahout shouted a different cry. The forty beaters on foot and the half dozen elephants paraded forward.

***

The Sutcliffes' ferry ride to Gauhati via the Brahmaputra River fell short of Mara's expectations. She hoped to see deadly crocodiles on the banks poised for ambush or a tiger emerging from the thicket. Instead, her only sight was the endless emerald jungle foliage broken by herders bathing their livestock or village women washing clothes, although the laughter of their children splashing in the shallows made her smile.

Shortly after arrival, her family checked into a hotel near St. Joseph's Cathedral. Afterward, she ventured alone to the main Gauhati market. The bazaar exceeded her expectations. It spilled across the dusty square in a jumble of stalls and mats, each crowded with bright bolts of cloth, brass trinkets, baskets of turmeric, ginger, and cardamom. Smoke from cooking fires mingled with the bite of mustard oil. With each step, Mara looked in a different direction. She breathed deeply through her nose as she strolled past the sweet scent of jaggery wafting from trays sitting on straw mats. Hawkers called in Hindi, Assamese, and clipped English; their voices tumbled over one another like the currents of the Brahmaputra River over boulders.

Mara wore a white cotton dress that extended to her wrists and ankles. Her grandmother's silver cross hung over her chest. Nonetheless, more than a few pedestrians turned their heads to look at her. Mara failed to notice them. She stopped in her tracks at the sight of a gaunt woman crouched at the market's edge with two children clinging to her rumpled sari. Their faces were smudged and their voices remained silent. Yet out of the throngs of souls bustling through the bazaar, Mara felt their large eyes connect with her. She paused. *At long last, my dream of shopping in the Gauhati Market and finding a colorful dress has come true. But can I ignore them? Would God bless my voice and hymn to hundreds at St. Joseph's Cathedral if I walk on?* Mara turned her head. This time, she spotted a dress of indigo Dhaka muslin shot through with silver thread. Her mind cleared as she walked over to look at it. The vendor, a seasoned man with a gray beard and wearing a turban, looked her over with widening gray eyes and licked his sun-chaffed lips.

Mara pointed to the dress.

He held it up before handing it to her.

He spoke to her in Hindi. "For you, my beautiful one, twelve rupees."

Mara blanched at the price. Her pupils dilated, and her eyelids slumped as she looked down at the dress.

"For such a lovely betiji, your happiness is more important than my profit." The left side of his mouth curled upward. "Ten rupees."

Should I? Mara closed her eyes and pinched her chin before biting her lower lip and speaking, "I have nine rupees. It's all I have." She held the dress close to her.

"I don't usually do this." The vendor folded his arms. "Nine it is."

Mara placed the dress on the table and reached for her purse. She glanced behind her. The woman with the toddler son and daughter remained in place but no longer looked at her. Her children clung to her mournfully as she held out a jittering right palm. The marketgoers passed her by without looking. Mara's jaw chattered as she reached into her purse. She pulled out a rupee. "Pardon me, sir." Mara walked over to a food stand and bartered for two bundles of banana leaf-wrapped sweet meat, rotis, and lentil cakes. She walked over to the indigent woman and pressed the warm bundles in her hands. The startled children looked up to her with open mouths and blinking eyelids. Mara smiled at them and playfully pinched their cheeks. With a soft lilt in her voice, she half hummed and half chuckled the hymn she would sing to hundreds in the Cathedral. The children laughed. Mara closed her eyes and saw a vision of an angel smiling upon her. The angel, without speaking, let Mara know that she had stirred the children's first laugh. The mother beamed at Mara. She smiled back, reached into her purse, and dropped several coins into the woman's cup.

Mara walked as though the Market Place's hard-packed earth had transformed into clouds. She faced the vendor.

"You claimed you had only nine rupees, but I saw you buy food from that vendor." He pointed to a food stand. "And then you gave the food and more of your money to the untouchable beggar. At nine rupees, I would make no profit selling you my most elegant and expensive dress. Now I know you can afford my asking price of twelve rupees."

"You know that I could never lie to a wise and crafty businessman like you, sir." Mara tightened her lips. "I only had nine rupees. Now I have even less." Mara took a deep breath and closed her eyes before looking upward with a smile, "Perhaps owning something so extravagant and impractical is not the Good Lord's will." She clutched her crucifix. "I do believe that you can sell me that carmine red and saffron yellow cotton dress with the block printed paisleys and climbing vines for a price beneficial to us both."

The vendor tensed his lips and looked Mara over. "Three rupees."

"How about two?" Mara smiled.

I never imagined such a lovely young lady could bargain like a hardened man." The vendor hesitated for five seconds before smiling back. "Two rupees it is."

After paying for the dress, the vendor handed it to her. Mara held it in front of her and smiled.

***

The procession of elephants and beaters reached a riverbank backed with three-meter-high Saccharum grass. Sir Nigel tapped the Mahout's shoulder. He turned his head to make eye contact with him. Browning snapped his fingers. The Mahout shouted and waved his arms. The other Mahouts stopped their elephants and formed a semicircle between the river and the Saccharum grass. Sir Nigel turned to Lawrence. "Now begins the waiting game. First, the beaters will flush the tiger out of the thicket into the clearing." Thirty-five men armed only with sticks, joined by five more men pounding on drums, invaded the thicket and thrashed aside the saccharum grass.

"Those men," Lawrence pointed to them, "are entering the tiger's lair unarmed. They're risking their lives and limbs while we sit on top of an elephant with high-powered rifles?" Lawrence furrowed his brow. "How is that a gentleman's sport?"

"Ahh…Mr. Mills," Browning's lips curled a fraction upward. "Even board chairman, military commanders, and royalty cower at my presence. Yet you confront me with questions. Let that serve as your first clue to why Kali and I have chosen you. You have much to learn about British and native ways. Let me teach you your first lesson. How many Pennsylvania Railroad workers lost their lives or limbs last year?"

57

Lawrence blushed. "One in nine, but we do everything possible to limit..."

Sir Nigel shot up his arm like a traffic cop directing traffic, palm forward, fingers together. "One in nine? And what's your risk, Mr. Mills?"

Lawrence bit his lip.

"Yet the rails are laid, the trains run, the profits increase, the board and investors are satisfied, and you and the workers get paid. You observe the railroad workers from a safe distance, and you get paid more than those risking life and limb. Why is that, Mr. Mills?" Sir Nigel narrowed his eyes and gazed sharply into Lawrence's eyes.

Lawrence took a deep breath. The pitch and volume of his voice dropped a notch. "Because of my education."

"Yes. Mr. Mills. The University of Pennsylvania. A fine institute, but an institution of high privilege, is it not?"

"Yes...But..."

"But nothing. Your family's wealth and position, as well as your hereditary intelligence and your personal diligence, keep you safe and comfortable."

Lawrence thought of George Cabot's disapproval of his family's wealth and position shortcomings. The words never formed in his throat.

"Mr. Mills, you learn quickly. You did choose to join my hunt." Sir Nigel raised his eyes. "If it would assuage your conscience, you may join the beaters."

Lawrence bit his lower lip before looking away from Nigel.

"I thought so, Mr. Mills. I hope soon you will choose just as wisely and join me and Kali and share our reign as Skanda and live with power and immortality."

The noise and sight of rustling Saccharum grass interrupted their conversation. Browning grabbed his .500 NE Westley Richards double-barreled rifle. He looked at Lawrence, frozen in place, and glowered at him. He grabbed the Winchester .405 bolt-action rifle and shoved it into Lawrence's arms. Browning raised his rifle, sight to his eye. Lawrence squeezed his rifle stock with almost enough firmness to leave a handprint. The rumbling earth and the threshing of grass reached a crescendo. The beaters scattered like ants after a boot stomped on their hill. Browning had his finger poised on his rifle's trigger. The seconds were taught as piano wire. *If we laid rails here,* Lawrence thought, *this would be an oncoming locomotive, not an animal.*

It emerged from the Saccharum grass. Its thick folds of gray skin looked like armor on a medieval warhorse. The horn extended from just above its nasal bone like a knight's lance. Nigel Browning muttered indecipherable curses as he lowered his weapon. "An Asian rhino is not what we came to hunt. We're out of range for our bullets to penetrate its armored hide." He shoved his weapon back on the rack. "Firing a non-fatal shot into the beast may provoke a charge and panic the elephants. Moreover, our gunfire will alert the tigers." He turned to Lawrence. "Do you have any idea of what the Chinese would pay for its horn?"

Lawrence shrugged.

"More than the crown is paying you for a year as Engineer in Charge of the Assam-Bengal Railway."

"They're almost gone. I've never seen a rhino. And you'd waste one for its horn?"

"The rhino is but a relic, like Shiva's bull Nandi. Kali will give me the spirit of the mightiest and fiercest beast and the power to rule them. Do not trouble me with extinction. Take that up with your President Roosevelt. Do not forget where you are, Mr. Mills. Here, I make beasts immortal by conquest. Even if killing the beast would've proven daunting, never doubt my capability as a hunter and a marksman. I used my power to spare the beast. Follow me, and I will grant you the same power over life and death."

Lawrence shifted his gaze from the plantation master's burning eyes to the rhinoceros, who now drank from the river. The next five minutes seemed to Lawrence like five years. The rhinoceros at last returned to the jungle.

Sir Nigel shouted in Assamese for the beaters, drummers, and elephant mahouts to return to their positions and resume the tiger hunt.

***

Mara stood alone in her hotel room, adjacent to her parents' room. She was two hours away from singing before hundreds of people in St. Joseph's Cathedral. On her bed lay her new red and saffron dress. She smiled, thinking, *I love the bright colors and the paisley and vine embroidery. It's delightful, and I can almost hear it whisper of my newfound freedom.* Next to it lay the lavender dress her father had given her. Mara pinched her chin and stared at the lavender dress with its lovely pintucks placed neatly across the bodice and its accompanying white sash. *It's more than a gift from my father. It's his way of telling me that I am no longer a little girl but a woman.* Mara dropped to her knees and prayed, "Lord Jesus, I ask in the name of the Father and the Holy Ghost that I may present myself in a way that glorifies not me but you. Let it be my song and not myself that draws attention and glorifies your name. May you use it to win new souls and strengthen the faith of those who already believe. Amen."

Mara placed her new saffron and red dress over her left forearm. She recalled her hard bargaining with the seasoned vendor before putting it back on her bed and picking up her father's lavender dress. Standing in front of the mirror, she held

60

her father's lavender dress in front of her and closed her eyes. Three seconds later, she hung the dress in the closet next to a third choice: her ankle and wrist-length white dress. *It's comfortable and modest, and it served me well in Sundarpur. But I'm in Gauhati, not Sundarpur, and I'm a woman now. It's my decision. I am singing as a guest at St. Joseph's Cathedral as a Baptist. Will Catholics be receptive to me and my hymn? Often have I been told of my natural outer beauty. Will that prove an asset or a distraction? I was invited to glorify God, not myself.* Mara donned the white dress. She clutched her grandmother's cross, kissed it, and wore it around her neck. She peered into the mirror and tapped a pinch of powder on her cheek from the compact that her father had given her.

***

The cathedral rose before her in a hush of stone and shadow. *Was it only days ago that I sang in our little, tin-roofed chapel in Sundarpur?* She looked up. *The cathedral's pointed arches seem to stretch Heavenward like hands in prayer.* Tall, narrow windows glimmered with saints caught in colored glass. From the rear entrance where she stood with her parents, Mara scanned the sweep of the nave and saw rows upon rows of polished hardwood pews under a towering, vaulted ceiling of hardwood ribs. The dark sheen of the hardwood's polish reflected lantern light. She turned to her parents. "Father, Mother, I know God would not have brought me here if he did not deem me ready. May he forgive me, for my faith falters. I'm scared." Mara touched her fingertips to her forehead. "I've never sung before a fraction of the people that will come to see and hear me. What if my voice can't fill such a huge cathedral? What if they disagree with the words of my song?"

"Oh, my beautiful daughter." Mara's mother placed her hands on Mara's shoulders. "You have already answered your question. God brought you here. He believes in you even more than you believe in him. He did not bring you here to fail, but to glorify his name." Leena kissed her daughter's cheek. "Trust in him."

61

"Mara," Reverend Brian Sutcliffe put one hand on Mara's and the other on his wife's shoulder. "This magnificent cathedral was built to God's glory. Your hymn and voice will do the same. We are in his holy presence. It is written in Mathew 18:20: For where two or three are gathered in thy name, I am present. Let us link hands and pray." The Sutcliffes linked hands. "Heavenly Father, in Jesus's name, let the Holy Spirit bolster Mara and give her the confidence to enable her gift of voice to glorify your name through her voice and the words of her hymn. Amen."

"Amen." Mara beamed. "Thank you, father. We have come a long way. It's too late to turn back now. I believe I can do this and do it to his glory."

***

Bishop Carlo Fregosi stood on the lectern, high above the Cathedral's standing room only gathering. "Dearly beloved in Christ, this morning we are graced with a guest from beyond our flock. Miss Mara Sutcliffe. God our father has blessed her with a voice most rare. Let us open our hearts, that the Holy Ghost may move us and unite us through her song, a song given to us for no other purpose than to honor our Lord Christ Jesus."

The choirmaster nodded to Mara. She closed her eyes and said a final prayer; *Lord be with me.* Her tingling nerves calmed with each step closer to the altar's center. She stood upon the choir steps and faced the congregation. Hundreds of blank faces stared back at her. Mara glanced at the Choirmaster. He nodded and waved his baton. She sang,

"You only live once, on this earthly shore,

Your soul is a treasure, worth so much more.

Though sorrows may stay, and years drift away,

One Savior has come to show you the way."

62

The choir sang,

> *"One life, then eternity,*
>
> *The cross has won our victory.*
>
> *Rejoice, he has paid the price,*
>
> *No second death, but eternal life."*

Mara sang,

> *"He calls the lost, through the darkest night,*
>
> *His mercy is strong; his love shines bright.*
>
> *The gate is narrow, but the shepherd will guide,*
>
> *His word shows the way; his arms open wide."*

The choir sang,

> *"One life, then eternity,*
>
> *The cross has won our victory.*
>
> *Rejoice, he has paid the price,*
>
> *No second death, but eternal life."*

Mara sang,

> *"When shadows falter, and dawn appears,*
>
> *He'll banish all pain and dry all our tears.*
>
> *A crown of life he will give to all who believe,*
>
> *and life without end, his children receive."*

Mara and the choir sang together. *"One life, then eternity,*

> *The cross has won our victory.*
>
> *All praise to the risen Son,*
>
> *The Lamb, our only One."*

Mara stood still, smiling at the congregation. They remained motionless and silent, as if unwilling to profane the moment. She spotted a few crossing themselves while others bowed their heads.

More than one discreetly wiped away their tears. The choirmaster's smile seemed wide enough to bridge the gap between Sundarpur and Gauhati or even childhood and adulthood. Mara made her graceful exit. Her parents waited for her in the sacristy. Leena cried openly. Brian beamed and embraced his daughter.

***

Browning had not addressed Lawrence since the rhinoceros returned unmolested to the thicket. He only dared to glance at Browning, who studied the jungle intensely. *What do I make of this man?'* Lawrence stole another peek at Sir Nigel. *How can he so cavalierly grant himself the decision of life or death as if flipping a coin?*

Browning broke the silence by murmuring something about Kali's patience. The clouds gathered low over the canopy, their rumble mixing with the restless growls of the elephants. Lawrence gazed at the Winchester .405 bolt-action rifle that Browning had assigned to him. *Is God, or gods as Browning puts it, still watching this place, or has the jungle chosen its own darker master?*

The jungle's tension drew tighter, like violin strings under a player's turning peg. The jungle's silence amplified the distant call of a peacock and the faint rasp of cicadas. The mahouts muffled their voices, steadying the now restless elephants. Browning handed Lawrence his rifle. Beaters shattered the hush by thrashing through the three-meter-tall Saccharum grass; drummers followed, banging a steady beat. The tiger burst from the thicket with a roar. It snapped its head back and forth, baring its teeth and growling menacingly at everything within its sight. The beaters, having accomplished their task, retreated. The elephants' trumpet blasts further enraged the beast. Sir Nigel narrowed his eyes and shouted, "Now, Mills!" Browning's glare burned through him.

64

Lawrence flinched at the command before firing. The rifle's scope cracked against his brow, the shot striking the tiger's shoulder. The beast roared- pain and fury fused- and sprang. It swatted the nearest beater's head with its paw and its unsheathed claws. The beater's bloodied head stayed on his neck, but hung there crooked, grotesque as a puppet's.

"Damn you, Mills!" Browning aimed for only a split second before shooting a bullet between the tiger's eyes. Browning lowered his rifle at port arms. "Now you know the true master of this domain." A slow, knowing grin tugged at one corner of his mouth. "Nevertheless, you didn't do half bad for a colonial."

Lawrence did not respond. He looked at the blood-drenched corpse of the fallen beater and turned pale. He closed his eyes and lowered his head.

"Do you think I can't read your mind, Mr. Mills?" Sir Nigel moved in front of Lawrence. "We came with forty beaters; we are leaving with thirty-nine. Let him serve as your first blood sacrifice to Kali. The blood of man nourishes her power and immortality. She will likewise reward your blood sacrifice by adopting you as her son and giving you power and immortality denied to mortal man." Nigel nodded toward the tiger and the fallen beater. "Come. We'll view our trophy."

***

Nigel and Lawrence joined the beaters surrounding the kill. "Even better," Nigel lowered his rifle. "The beast is a male. A dealer will meet me at the Sundarpur docks. The Chinese pay handsomely for such parts."

Three minutes later, other members of the hunting party had dismounted and joined Sir Nigel.

Railway Board Chairman clapped Browning's shoulder with a nervous laugh. "Splendid shot, Sir Nigel, a clean strike under pressure."

65

Colonel Hutchins nodded briskly, "Textbook, sir. My men could learn a thing or two from your skill and composure."

Prince Alaric removed his hat and smiled faintly. "Most impressive. You command the hunting instincts of a grand master, Sir Nigel. You do credit to your country in general and Englishmen in particular."

The hunting party dispersed to their howdahs. Sir Nigel grabbed Lawrence's arm to prevent him from following them. After they had boarded their howdahs, Sir Nigel spoke, "You wear your thoughts too openly, Mr. Mills. I must teach you the virtue of British stoicism. The fallen beater troubles you still." Browning gestured toward the lifeless man. "Leave him where he lies. His end serves as part of the circle. Now you will speak your first invocation to Kali. We now shall complete your sacrifice to the highest Goddess." Nigel Browning raised his eyes to the clouds above. "Oh, Kali of flame and shadow, of divine power and immortality, accept the blood of this man. Bind the living and the dead in your eternal circle." He narrowed his eyes, furrowed his brow, and gazed into Lawrence's eyes. "Repeat it, Mr. Mills."

Lawrence's lips moved without uttering a sound.

***

The launch steamer puffed towards its Sundarpur destination, its paddlewheel adding more ripples and eddies to the roil of the Brahmaputra River. Mara sat on the upper deck beneath a sagging canvas awning, her hymn still echoing in her mind. The Bishop and choirmaster had seconded what she felt from the Holy Spirit. Her performance and the words of her hymn were a triumph beyond herself.

A village of bamboo huts, palm groves, and their women washing clothes while their children frolicked in the shallows, interrupted the omnipresent jungle. Soon, the forest reasserted its emerald dominance, spiced with blazing red palash, crimson hibiscus, and purple orchids. Mara detected a rustling in the grass before spotting orange and black. A tiger emerged from the thicket. Even in its relaxed jaunt to the riverbank, Mara could see its muscles rippling with each step. The cat looked up before drinking. Mara looked directly into its eyes. *Why do I not fear you? How beautiful and mighty you are. How glorious is God's creation?* Mara continued to look back as the boat chugged toward Sundarpur. She got a final glimpse of the tiger returning to its realm. Steepling her hands, she prayed, "Lord Jesus, I thank you for letting me witness the beauty of your creation. Before sin entered the world, even the mighty were gentle. Keep me as your servant up to and beyond the day that you make all things new, when the tiger will lie down with the lamb."

***

Sir Nigel waited on the Sundarpur wharves for his Chinese dealer's launch steamer to arrive from Gauhati. He held it in a sealed box. Rahman, his bodyguard and bearer, stood next to him, his hand poised on his tulwar sword's lacquered scabbard. *The Chinese. How pathetic their primitive superstitions and foolish nostrums. Their ignorance amuses me, but their gold delights. A Chinaman can stand on another Chinaman's shoulders and still not reach my stature. A rhino horn for virility and a tiger penis for power?"* Browning sniggered. *I put a tiger's manhood in this box. A Chinaman will soon put money in my pockets. Their ignorance costs them more than they will ever know. True manhood is only found through the most intimate dance with Kali. Once I am united with her, no man will match my virility, and my power will have no limit.*

***

The launch steamer nudged against the Sundarpur jetty. A sailor dropped the gangplank, and the passengers disembarked. Sir Nigel lingered on the dock, waiting for his dealer. He watched a woman exit. Her cotton carmine red and saffron yellow dress

67

with paisleys and climbing vines fluttered in the breeze. A gentle gust rustled her flowing black hair. Each of her ethereal steps stirred a vision and sound in Browning's mind: orchestration, voices, and theatrics. Wagner's Tristan reached for Isolde through the night and sang of his unresolved longing. *A gentleman's decorum be damned! I am possessed! I cannot look away.* His focus cut through her like a blade- steady, surgical, unblinking. He handed Rahman the box with the tiger part and spoke without looking away from Mara. "The Chinese think medicine made from a tiger will perfect them as a man. Yet it's the divine feminine and her purity that will ascend me to godhood."

Mara cringed. *The tall Western man is handsome, but his eyes are a window to Hell. The huge Assamese wearing a turban scares me as well.* A memory from ten years ago flashed in her mind. Each of her steps crunched dry twigs and leaves. She tripped over a log and stumbled. After regaining her balance, a foreboding beset her. She turned with trepidation. The king cobra's hood was flared; it raised its body in a vertical S, coiled to strike.

It lifted its head high enough to look directly into her eyes. Its eyes held no malice. Mara knew to freeze in place. Fear overwhelmed her thoughts to the point that she couldn't even pray. After three eternal seconds, the cobra lowered its head, no longer wary of Mara. It turned with a slow ripple and slithered back into the brush. This time, Mara froze in place in the gangway's center. A Chinese man wearing an ankle-length blue silk robe under a short black jacket jostled her. He moved with the calm precision of a man who had weighed every bargain before striking it. Mara watched him as he approached the handsome but menacing Caucasian. The Chinese man tipped his head slightly and folded his hands in front of him.

Mara's parents caught up to her on the gangway. She grabbed her father's arm and whisked her parents to the awaiting oxen-led bullock cart. She didn't dare so much as glance back at the tall, handsome, but sinister man.

Chapter 10

Sledgehammers rang against spikes, sharp and steady, making Lawrence's ears throb. Ahead lay virgin forest waiting for his railway path to tame. Lawrence set up his theodolite ahead of the Assamese trackmen. He peered through the scope and saw a thick banyan tree in its crosshairs. *The tree is blocking the straightest path. Do we lose time and exhaust our workers by clearing it out of the way, or do we go around it and use extra rails to build an unnecessary curve?* Lawrence stepped back and opened his pocket watch. The midday sun gleaming on its silver case told the time better than the watch's hands. *I'll eat lunch over that decision.* Lawrence walked over to the Sirdar. "Break the workers for lunch." The Sirdar blew into his Pepa horn loud enough to override the cacophony of spikes. The workers dropped their sledgehammers, machetes, and axes in place. The pounding and clanging of metal against metal still rang in Lawrence's ears.

He waved to Corporal Stanton. The soldier held up his Tiffen carrier and flashed the sun off its tin case, signaling for him to join him for lunch. Lawrence left his theodolite in place, secured his horse, and walked toward the Corporal. Weeds clung to his boots and muffled his steps. *Both the jungle and the work site have fallen oddly silent. Has the racket of trackmen hammering spikes wrecked my hearing, or is it something else? A foreboding?* He stepped on something that felt different than a weed, twig, or branch. A two-decade-old memory flashed in his mind. Lawrence was playing in his backyard. The Pennsylvania summer's midday heat matched this Assamese summer afternoon. Young Lawrence pressed his foot on top of his family's BF Goodrich rubber garden hose. After building sufficient pressure, he would release his foothold and drench his playmates. Lawrence remembered the time when his foot slipped off the hose. The water pressure caused it to swing wildly and strike his shin with the metal end…

…Lawrence felt a sting just above his boot. He reflexively raised his foot off the cylindrical object. The object was alive. It spread its hood. A second later, its rusty gray body slithered into the grass. He raised a trouser leg and saw two pinpricks in his right calf.

"Stay where you are!" Corporal Stanton shouted to him. "Sit down and don't move a muscle!" He trotted on his horse to Lawrence. "I saw what happened. Based on the V pattern on its hood, you took a bite from a common Indian cobra. I know it's easy for me to say, but try to relax. We'll pull you through this."

"I'm fine. I don't feel anything yet."

"Yet." He tightened his lips and furrowed his brow in concern. "Unfortunately, you'll soon feel the symptoms. Trust us to get you through this." Corporal Stanton put two fingers in his mouth and blasted a whistle. Another soldier on horseback galloped over to them. "Sergeant Barry!" Stanton shouted! "It's a cobra bite!"

The soldier dismounted. He unbuckled the khaki pouch from his belt; the stenciled letters, 'R.A.M.C.', were nearly worn away. Inside lay rolls of gauze, a brown glass bottle, a length of rubber tubing, and a clasping string of webbing. He spotted the double pinprick wound on Lawrence's right leg. "Hold still, sir." Sergeant Barry stood over Lawrence. "I can see that your eyelids are starting to droop. How is your vision?"

"Blurry," Lawrence answered.

"That's the first symptom, sir." The sergeant bit his lower lip. "I'm afraid it's no dry bite. Let's hope the snake didn't inject a full dose of venom. We'll stabilize you here and get you to a clinic in Sundarpur. Have faith. We'll pull you through this." He wound a canvas sheet with a rubber strap above the dual pinprick wounds. "I know this feels uncomfortable. It's needed to slow your circulation and keep the venom from spreading."

"Do…Do…Do…What you have to do." Lawrence answered with slurred speech.

Sergeant Barry cut a small cross over the wound and spat on it. "Let's hope this old way works until we can get you to a proper clinic."

"We know of a clinic in nearby Sundarpur." Corporal Stanton raised his hands. "Let's get him there post haste." He looked at the Assamese supervisor. "Sirdar!" He whistled. "Have the workers clear that bullock cart and bring it over here. We must get this man to Sundarpur and fast!"

***

Workers threw railway supplies and tools out of the bullock cart. An Assamese cart driver drove the dual-oxen-led bullock cart over to Lawrence and the British soldiers. Sergeant Barry and Corporal Stanton lifted Lawrence and eased him into the cart. Stanton jumped in and shouted to the driver, "Sundarpur! Now!"

***

Corporal Stanton wiped his brow with a damp rag. "Stay with me, mate, we're arriving in Sundarpur." Lawrence breathed in gasps, his consciousness wavering between reality and hallucination…*He was back home in Wayne, Pennsylvania. The year was 1895, and Lawrence was a sturdy youth with his entire life before him. His schooling had taken on purpose as his dreams were within reach. He sat on a curved bench sided with carved ornamentation and rested his feet on the recently constructed train station's floor of vitrified bricks laid in a running board pattern. The Wayne train station's two Victorian structures flanked the quadruple-tracked Pennsylvania Railroad. Its two-story Victorian square tower with a pyramidal turret stood as a graceful miniature of Wayne's baronial homes. He looked westward. Smoke billowed above the oak and birch trees that grew beside the tracks. The sound of the chugging locomotive and the tooting of its whistle preceded its circling the bend and coming into view. Lawrence waved to the locomotive engineer. He waved back as his train bolted past…*

…Lawrence gasped for breath and clenched his jaw as a sharp wave of pain in his right leg ended his daydream. "It's all right, mate." Corporal Stanton put a damp rag on his sweaty forehead and tightened the tourniquet around his leg by pulling on its runner strap. The Corporal noticed increased blackening and swelling at the bite site…Lawrence's mind drifted…*Fires, flames, heat- the inferno was everywhere. Rocks too sharp to rest upon glowed red hot. His throat was too parched to scream for water, water, but there was no water. Sir Nigel Browning appeared before him. His crimson complexion and pronounced brow ridge blurred his otherwise handsome features.* "You had your chance. I am now Shiva. Kali and I offered to adopt you as our son, Skanda. Kali would have bestowed you with immortality. You would have led our army of destruction and helped rule the renewed Earth. Now you are but a prisoner in this eternal realm of darkness and flame."

***

Mara faced her class. She pointed to a chalkboard with the arithmetic multiplication tables. "We will learn our tables by singing them. I will sing first, and you sing back to me." Mara beamed at the children and sang while pointing to the matching numbers. "One times one is one; the planting is done. Two times two is four, the seed's grown more." Mara nodded to the class.

The children sang, "One times one is one, the planting is done. Two times two is four, the seed's grown more."

Mara sang, "Three times three is nine, its branches grow with time. Four times four is sixteen. Its trunk grows thick and lean."

The children sang, "Three times three is nine, its branches grow with time. Four times four is sixteen. Its trunk grows thick and lean."

***

Lawrence heard Mara and the children sing. A wave of Euphoria vanquished the stygian. He now rested in a cloud. A bright light filtered through the haze.

"Stop." Corporal Stanton yelled at the carter. "Here's the dispensary. Help me carry him inside. The cart driver and the corporal carried Lawrence in a stretcher. They ran him into the dispensary and rolled him onto a bed.

***

A local bystander ran into the school. "Mara! Come quickly! There's an emergency! You're needed in the dispensary."

"I'm sorry, class. You're dismissed for the day. We'll pick up where we left off tomorrow morning."

The children groaned before they left the schoolhouse.

Mara ran into the dispensary.

Corporal Stanton walked up to her. "Miss Sutcliffe. It's our American Engineer in Chief. A cobra bit him."

I recognize him, but from where? She ran to him and held his hand. It was meant to comfort, yet something moved within her, something new, something different, something beyond a nurse's compassion.

Lawrence saw her face emerging from the light. Waves of comfort surged from his hand to his mind. "Kali. You've come to save me after all."

Mara blanched and released his hand. She took a deep breath before smiling at him. "No. I am not Kali." She re-took his hand. "And Jesus Christ is the only name under heaven that a man can be saved."

73

He looked deeply into her large brown eyes. He saw a window to something unknown. "You're an angel. You've come to take me to God. I am not ready. Don't make me go back to that horrible place."

"I am not an angel either. I am Mara. Your nurse."

Mara? That name? That lovely face. Where? Lawrence's mind went blurry.

"With the help of our Lord God Jesus Christ, we will get you through this." She tightened her lips. "You probably can't understand me in your delirium, but you're conscious and breathing." She looked at his leg and spoke. "The bite area is swollen and discolored. So far, there's no sign of infection. Better it be a cobra bite." She looked at Corporal Stanton. "A bite from a Russell's viper is far more painful and would've put him in danger of losing his leg. You did a fine job with the tourniquet. Corporal. Please get me some carbolic acid from that cabinet and a pitcher of water."

Douglas Stanton loped over, grabbed a bottle of carbolic acid and a water pitcher, and ran back to Mara. "Here!"

"Put it on the table." She poured water into a glass, placed her hand behind Lawrence's head, and helped him drink. After returning the glass to the table, she poured the carbolic acid onto a cotton swab and rubbed it into the snake bite wound. "I see you already made an incision and tried to suck out the venom. Good work, corporal. Your fast and efficient first aid has bettered his odds."

"I know this is not the place to say it, but I have attended your father's church services. I have seen and heard you sing. Your voice is heavenly, and you are beautiful. I always hoped to meet you, just not under these circumstances."

Mara blushed and looked away. "Now I remember him." She looked at Lawrence. "He's the handsome man who accompanied you."

Handsome…Hmm. "His name is Lawrence. He's the Engineer and Chief of the Assam-Bengal Railway. He's from America. At first, I resented having to work under a Yankee civilian, but he proved a sound fellow after all. I know you will do everything possible for him."

"Of course I will. I will need help from the Lord above. Please retrieve some quinine from the cabinet to add to this pitcher of water. I promise not to leave his side."

"Mara!" Reverend Brian Suttcliffe burst into the dispensary. "What's going on?"

Corporal Stanton answered before Mara could speak. "It's the American Engineer in Chief. A cobra bit him."

"We only have the basics to treat the symptoms. I will run to the telegraph station and send an urgent wire to every station along the line. Cobra anti-venom is hard to find, but surely between here and Calcutta, someone will have it. Before I go, let's all say a quick prayer. Brian took his daughter's hand. She took Lawrence's hand. Corporal Stanton completed the link. "Dear Heavenly Father, in the name of Jesus and the Holy Ghost, please comfort and watch over Lawrence. May we find anti-venom, and may it arrive fast while your healing hand restores Lawrence's health. Amen."

Brian, Mara, and Stanton repeated "Amen." Lawrence only saw Mara's visage framed in light. He closed his eyes and slept.

***

The sun slid under the horizon. Dusk gave way to night. The darkness flowed into Sundarpur like a liquid. One oil lamp cast a shadowy light in the clinic. Mara stayed behind after the others had gone. She wiped sweat from Lawrence's brow with a damp cloth. She couldn't help but notice the strength in his square jaw and the gentleness in his round cheeks. She clasped his right hand. "Lord, forgive me if what I feel is wrong." She added her left hand, enclosing his hand in both of hers. "Lord Jesus, let his fear, distress, and confusion drain into me." Mara bent over and kissed his forehead.

…Lawrence stood with Dorothy on the pier in New York. The RMS Oceanic transatlantic liner towered above them. The smoke and steam plumes from her twin funnels mingled with the morning fog. Dorothy looked dreamlike in the haze. A wisp of blonde hair escaped from her dove gray hat, crowned with a pale ostrich plume. Her tailored traveling coat hugged her figure. Yet soon her radiance would fade to memory. "I will miss you terribly, Lawrence, but I know this is best for our future."

"I don't want to say goodbye, but I must. My sadness is only eased because we both know that this is the only way I can make your journey from a Cabot to a Mills move in the right direction."

Dorothy saw moisture in his eyes. It was no match for her tears. She leaned forward. Their lips met, and their tongues mingled for a final time.

As the tugboats pulled RMS Oceanic from the docks along the Hudson toward its transatlantic journey, Lawrence got a last view of her white-gloved hand waving farewell.

Dorothy. Dorothy. You were my every waking and sleeping thought during my endless journey to Assam, and you still dominate my thoughts now that I have arrived. Two porters in loose cotton dhotis hoisted his trunk from the bullock cart and carried it up the verandah steps. A lean man in a turban and white tunic, his newly assigned bearer, followed with his suitcase. He opened the door and, with a sweep of his arms, said, "Your quarters, Sir." The porters followed and placed his trunk in front of an iron-framed bed. It sat on the bedside table. A letter. 'It's from Dorothy.' Lawrence ran over and tore it open…

… "No! No!" Lawrence awoke screaming. "You can't do this to me, no Dorothy, no!"

"It's all right." Mara hugged him. "Everything will be fine." She patted his back. "Let me take care of you, and with the Good Lord's help, you'll get better in no time."

Lawrence returned her embrace. They held each other for five seconds. Afterward, Lawrence managed to sit up in bed. *I'm dying. I know I'm dying. God would only send someone so lovely to comfort a dying man. She is either Kali or an Angel from Presbyterian Heaven.*

Mara blushed. *His blue eyes are clear. They now hold wonder.* "A cobra bit you, Lawrence. I would be lying if I told you your life was not in danger. I can see in your eyes that your symptoms are improving. My father is doing everything possible to find anti-venom. Until then, we will stay in prayer. I can only treat your symptoms to the best of my ability, and the medicine we have in the dispensary. But Heaven is unlimited. May your healing continue with this psalm. Mara held his hand and sang to him. "All praises to God who forgives all our sins and heals our ills. He redeems our life from destruction and crowns us with loving kindness and tender mercies."

Lawrence saw the oil lamp flicker light over her mahogany hair, turning the darkness to bronze in fleeting flashes. Shadows danced golden on her cheeks. Her eyes were a window to a better place, where he did not know. Her voice covered him in a wave of comfort. Lawrence fell into a deep slumber. Mara remained by his bedside.

***

Reverend Brian Sutcliffe rushed into the dispensary. He saw his daughter leaning toward Lawrence, holding his right hand with both of hers. "Mara?" She looked up at him. He noticed the dark circles beneath her bloodshot eyes.

"He's sleeping, Father."

Lawrence started to wake up. *The beautiful young woman who sang to me.* His arm felt like it weighed a ton as he reached up and touched Mara's cheek. "I'm not dreaming, and I'm not dead."

"No, Sir, you're very much alive." Brian walked over to Lawrence. "The fact that you're still alive means you have crossed the roughest waters. On average, a bite from a common Indian cobra takes nine hours to kill a man. Anti-venom is a recent discovery, so it's rare. My daughter may have told you that I have sent wires as far as Calcutta. With God's help, we will find you a dose. Until then, we will do what we can to treat the symptoms and keep you alive. It will require prayer as well as your inner strength."

Lawrence mumbled, "You're the American minister that my friend, the British Corporal, told me about."

"Yes. I am. I am Reverend Brian Sutcliffe. I am an ordained Baptist minister and missionary. I am originally from Baw-ston."

"Of course, that accent gives you away. You're a true Yankee. I am from Philadelphia."

"Philadelphia? Don't worry, I won't hold that against you. I don't meet many other Americans here in Raj, India. Even though you're a Brotherly Lovelander and Cradle-of-Liberty second cousin, you're an American. The spirit that beat the British Empire and tamed a frontier lives within you, Mr. Mills. Providence sent you here with a purpose. Your work with him is unfinished. With the help of God and my daughter Mara's care, you will pull through."

"With God's help, I will make sure of it." Mara squeezed Lawrence's hand and gazed at him raptly.

Brian hinted at a tight smile. Leena ran into the dispensary. She stopped in her tracks at the sight of Mara holding Lawrence's hand and staring fondly at him.

"Yes. Mara. Of course, you're Mara. I heard you sing during a Sunday service at your chapel. I was enchanted. You stayed on my mind."

"I saw you among the crowd, Lawrence. I hope the Lord that I sang of and put in your mind will come into your heart."

"I have much to consider. I'm feeling tired, Mara. I want to sleep."

Mara kept his hand in his. She sang to him Schubert's Wiegenlied, her voice as soft as the murmur of the oil lamp. "Schlafe, schlafe, holder suber Knabe, Leise wiegt dich deiner Mutter Hand…"

As Lawrence dozed off to Mara's voice. Brian put his arm around his wife and held her. Leena remained tense as the song soothed Lawrence.

***

Curtains shielded the morning sun. Sir Nigel continued to sleep. Banging on his door woke him.

"I'm sorry, sir." Rahman's voice boomed through the teak door. "I would never wake you up unless it were of vital importance. We got both unexpected news and the information you are waiting for."

"After I get dressed, I'll call for you to see me in the parlor. You two," he turned to Anjali and Layla. "Get dressed, prepare my morning tea, and bring it to the parlor." He snapped his fingers. "Now!"

***

79

He sat with an ankle resting on his knee. Anjali and Layla entered wearing matching saris of pale gold silk; their shoulders were modestly veiled, yet the folds clung closely. The fine fabric caught the morning sun like water over skin. They delivered Browning's morning tea with rehearsed sensual grace. He took a cup of tea from Anjali's tray. Layla placed a saucer on the table. Browning snapped his fingers. Bells around each of their ankles sounded their departure. Browning sipped his tea before nodding to Rahman.

His bodyguard and bearer read from a paper slip. "It's about the American railway engineer, Lawrence Mills. A cobra bit him. He is at the American missionary dispensary in Sundarpur. Their minister, a Reverend Brian Sutcliffe, is desperately searching for anti-venom."

Sir Nigel put his tea in the saucer, sat up straight, and planted both feet on the floor. "That's bad news. I have high hopes for the American. I possess anti-venom. Get a vial from the surgery room and have Nabin deliver it to the Sundarpur missionary dispensary immediately."

"Sir. There's more. It's about the woman at the Sundarpur dock…"

"She is no woman." Browning prodded at Rahman. "Do not ever refer to her as a woman. That is blasphemy. She is a goddess. She is Kali incarnate. Did my people find her?"

"Yes, sir." Rahman took a deep breath and considered the seriousness of Browning's demeanor. "Um, yes, sir, um, her given human name is Mara."

"Mara." Browning pinched his cheek. "Where is she?"

"How can I say this, Sir?" Rahman bit his lower lip. "Her mortal father is an American Baptist missionary. Her mortal mother is Assamese. She is caring for your American protégé at the dispensary. They are desperate for your anti-venom, sir."

"Hmm…Sir Nigel stood and pinched his chin. What is bad in the eyes of man is good for us. Our beloved goddess Kali will soon arrive in the flesh. Alert Nabin. Write him a letter explaining that we have anti-venom, but Mr. Sutcliffe, his wife, and their daughter, the Goddess, must come here in person to obtain it. Nabin will deliver the note." Browning put his hands on his hips. "Have our driver harness a team of our four swiftest horses to my carriage. I want Mara in my presence without delay. I want to meet her now. Kali will only take possession of her in my presence. Moreover, we can't let Mr. Mills's human form die before Kali and me, the reborn Shiva, adopt him as Skanda. In the meantime, go to the telegraph shed and have my operator send a message to Sundarpur. Ensure that the Sutcliffes know that they can't refuse my invitation." Browning snapped his fingers. Rahman wrote the note, put it into an envelope, and fulfilled his master's orders.

Chapter 11

Early Fall had broken the worst of the Assamese Summer heat. The punka-wallah kept the punka fan churning above Lawrence. Mara wiped sweat from Lawrence's brow with a damp cloth. "You have a fever. That is to be expected. The bite wound is still swollen and dark, but it isn't getting worse. That is a good sign." Mara grasped Lawrence's hand and held it.

"My vision is blurry, and my hearing is jumbled. Yet through this pain and suffering, I can behold your beauty and soothing voice. The touch of your hand is unmistakable. I would betray God Himself if I were not to fight for my life with everything I can muster. Besides, my leg better not get any worse." Lawrence managed to chuckle. "As well as you sing and as delightful your touch, I can't imagine you cutting off my leg with a bone saw."

Mara laughed. "King Solomon said in Proverbs, 'A merry heart does good like medicine, but a broken spirit dries the bones. You'd better keep on laughing, so I won't need that bone saw." Mara squeezed his hand. "Keep God in your corner while you fight the good fight. I expect nothing less." Mara leaned over and kissed his forehead.

Lawrence smiled, closed his eyes, and slept.

Mara continued to hold his hand. She closed her eyes and moved her lips in prayer. The racket of multiple hooves, bells, and a cracking whip clashing with panicked people, fowl, and goats interrupted her. She walked outside and saw a carriage drawn by four horses stop in front of her house. A thin Assamese boy jumped out of the carriage, ran up to their front door, and banged on it hard enough to rattle its hinges. Her father answered the door. She couldn't understand the boy's words, but by flaying his arms and bouncing on the balls of his feet, he conveyed that he had important news. She walked closer and overheard her father telling the boy something about not receiving a telegraph message. "Mara!" Her father called out to her. "Come quickly!" Mara sensed his urgency and sprinted over. "They've found anti-venom! This boy asks that we come as a family to the Browning tea plantation to get it."

Leena came to the door. "Leena. Come with us," Brian tilted his head to the carriage. "We need to go to the Browning estate. Sir Nigel has a vial of cobra anti-venom."

Brian, Leena, and Mara boarded the carriage with the young messenger. Little was spoken, although Mara felt tension from her mother. They made eye contact. Leena held her gaze. "Mara. I am both a woman and your mother. I can tell you have feelings for the stricken American. Yes, he is handsome, and I have heard only good things about him. Love is not sinful if you honor God's commandments. The book of James tells us that our faith justifies us to God, but our works justify us to our fellow man." Her expression softened. She smiled, reached out, and touched her daughter's leg. "I met your father while a student at Bethane. Yet we were never allowed to walk with a man, not even a classmate. A single glance could cost a girl her place. The matrons watched everything: who we spoke to, how long, and why. That may sound foolish and oppressive now, but the world hasn't changed as much as you think. A woman alone is still judged by the eyes that follow her." She winked. "But I still managed to marry your father after I graduated."

"What your mother is trying to say is that we approve of Lawrence." Brian smiled at his daughter. "But you need to follow our lead and show restraint. We have invested years in building our ministry through our chapel, school, and dispensary. An indiscretion with a man can undo everything that we've accomplished and bring God's work to a halt before you can say Jack Robinson."

***

The carriage sped along the driveway to Sir Nigel's mansion. "I have heard so much about this man, Sir Nigel Browning," Brian said. "I have never met him. I can't be anything other than impressed at the scale of his plantation. He employs more of Sundarpur's citizens than even the Bengal-Assam railway, so having rare cobra anti-venom does not surprise me."

"Mara," Leena pointed out of the window. "Look at his mansion. I've never seen anything like it, even near Calcutta."

Mara's eyes opened wide on first spotting the Browning mansion. Raised on a plinth, colonnaded verandas circled the structure. It had tall, shuddered sash windows and a high-pitched, gabled roof extended with wide eaves.

The carriage stopped under a portico of Corinthian columns. Rahman opened the door for them. *He's the man from the docks. Why does he have no expression? He's twice my father's size. I see nothing friendly in his eyes. What if he means us harm?*

"This way." Rahman pointed at the front door. Another servant opened the door. Rahman led them down a dimly lit hallway.

Mara looked upward. *Those hunting trophies, they look less like animals and more like furry tombstones.* On entering the drawing room, Mara gasped.

Sir Nigel stood erect as a general before the king. His gaze fixed upon her. *She is a beauty beyond an artist's reach. A Swami can try to tell us of the highest Satya-loka heaven, but now I stand in its essence. She is not human. She is Kali herself. Her dark hair foretells destruction. Her fair skin renewal. And within her earth-colored eyes lies a story untold.*

His gaze held Mara like a snare. His sharp brow ridges framed his eyes like casings holding bullets. She put her hand over her grandmother's cross, as if his stare alone could melt it, and pressed her chest to muffle the sound of her beating heart. Nervous energy surged to her legs. *I want to run, but where? I can't let my fear put Lawrence's life at risk.* She at last gathered her thoughts. *Lord Jesus, protect me.* Mara looked away.

She fears me. Good. Rather fear and respect than love and adoration. She does not know her identity. Kali sleeps within her soul. Soon, Mara will intimately know her. When Kali awakens within her, she will know I am Shiva. She will love and adore me as her divine husband. Together we shall rule for eternity. Until then, I must remain a refined gentleman. Starring is unbecoming. "I am Sir Nigel Browning. The owner of this plantation. You are the Reverend Sutcliffe, the American missionary, I presume."

"Yes, Sir, I am." Brian extended his hand. "I am originally from Boston."

Sir Nigel lowered his eyes and tilted his head downward at him while shaking his hand with a fraction more force and length than he expected. "Mrs. Sutcliffe, Miss Sutcliffe. Word of the American Engineer's misfortune has reached me. Dare I say his misfortune is my fortune as it brings exquisite grace to my home." He delicately kissed Leena's hand before tilting his head to Mara. "Have a seat." Browning pointed to three high-backed chairs. He spotted Brian lowering himself. "Ladies first, Reverend Sutcliffe."

***

Browning sat with the Sutcliffe family. He placed his ankle on his knee. Rather than face the room, he angled himself toward Mara. *'Try not to stare.'* He cautioned himself. *She is not yet ready to be worshiped.* "I am certain you know how many families depend on my wages. I have more acreage than entire counties in England and the United States. I can show you the new railway spur to my new factories and warehouses. Once the railway is finished and my operation is connected to the Port of Chittagong, I will control all the tea in the Northeast Asian subcontinent." *Stop boasting. It's vulgar and unbecoming. I can romance and woo any mortal woman on Earth. She is Kali, a Goddess. Trying to impress her is profane. Once Kali awakens*

85

 "And speaking of tea, how rude of me." They heard the tinkling of ankle bells. "Here comes our service now."

Mara squirmed as Browning's presence kept her ensnared. Leena became agitated at the sight of Anjali and Layla. They were dressed in matching black silk clinging close to their bodies, one with a red pallu and red pleats, and the other with green. Their perfumed scent was stronger than anything Leena had ever encountered on a woman. Layla placed her tray on a table and served Leena with exaggerated and practiced feminine movements and gestures. Anjali stood between Mara and Browning, shielding her from his sight. She made eye contact with Mara, winked, and licked her upper lip before moving her leg under the table and slyly rubbing her bare ankle on Mara's bare ankle. The brief, gentle friction nauseated Mara. Brian Sutcliffe noticed his wife and daughter's discomfort. "I greatly appreciate your hospitality. Your operation and estate are impressive indeed, and I thank you on behalf of many for providing jobs and wages. Nevertheless, a man's life hangs in the balance. You summoned us because you have cobra anti-venom. If you would, may you dispatch with it now and let us tend to our patient?"

Browning snapped his fingers twice. Layla and Anjali retreated to the kitchen. Their ankle bells signaled their departure. Browning touched his fingers in a steeple. "You're also American. Mr. Mills has the same spirit that ejected our empire a century and a quarter ago, vanquished marauding savages, and tamed a vast wilderness. Why do you underestimate him? Do you lack faith in your God? If your God is all mighty as you claim, won't he keep the American alive for an extra hour?" Sir Nigel lowered his hands. "I can see Miss Sutcliffe's discomfort. You saw our overhead water tank; I also have a new water closet." Sir Nigel stood. "It's down the hallway past the kitchen. I can have my bearer, Rahman, escort you."

Mara turned pale and shook her head.

"No. She will be fine." Brian smiled at his daughter.

Mara walked down the hallway. She smelled curry and mutton from the kitchen. *What strange noises. It sounds as though the cooks are devouring their own fare.* Curiosity made her look into the kitchen. She blanched. Anjali had Layla pinned into a corner. Her legs were wrapped around Anjali's waist, and her hands around the back of her neck, tighter than petal vines around the trunk of an areca palm. Anjali's hands braced Layla's buttocks as if to prevent fruit from falling off a branch. Their lips were combined with open mouths. Mara marched back to the parlor. Sweat ran down her pale face.

"What's wrong?" Leena leapt up and embraced her daughter. "What's wrong?"

Mara sobbed, tears joined her sweat as she embraced her mother.

"Sir," Brian spread his open palms. "Please. My daughter has taken ill. As much as we appreciate your hospitality, could you give us what we came for and excuse us?"

"Very well," A faint grin emerged on Browning's face, a soft snigger from his throat, "Reverend. I'll give you a chance to make it up to me later. First, have you and your family pose for a photograph with me, then I'll give you the anti-venom and have my carriage and driver return you to Sundarpur in plenty of time to administer the serum to Mr. Mills." Browning nodded to Brahman.

Brahman returned with their photographer. He set up the camera on a wooden and brass tripod. It stood in breathless silence. Its bellows extended like a predatory insect. Mara felt like a condemned convict standing on a gallows trap door. With a blinding flash, it was over.

"After it's developed, I will have my messenger bring you a copy. I will put mine in a suitable frame and have it join my gallery. Rahman," Browning nodded to his bearer and bodyguard. "Give them what they came for."

Brahman handed Brian a glass vial. "Escort them to my carriage and order the driver to return them to Sundarpur."

During the return journey, the Sutcliffes rode in silence, each lost in thoughts they dared not speak. The carriage wheels and horse hooves joined the rhythm of the jungle beyond. Mara dozed fitfully. She dreamed of herself in Biblical times. Angry villagers were dragging her through dust and dirt. *No. No. Lord, no.* She snapped out of her funk and said, "Father, mother, will you please pray with me? Lord, forgive and cleanse me with your holy blood. Forgive me for entering that realm of evil. Please understand that we needed the anti-venom to save Lawrence's life. Please bless and keep Lawrence until our return. Amen."

Brian and Leena repeated, "Amen."

Browning's manor vanished into the mist. Yet its presence lingered, like a scent the wind would never carry away.

Chapter 12

Mara exited the carriage first. She sprinted into the dispensary. "Lawrence! Lawrence!" She grabbed his hand and twice kissed his cheek. "Thank you, Lord Jesus, you're alive."

"I don't know if something better than your kiss awaits in the next life. Nevertheless, it's every reason on Earth to stay alive in this one."

"And you're going to live!" Mara's smile glowed like molten gold. "We got it!" Her eyes twinkled. "The anti-venom."

Brian followed her into the dispensary. "Here it is." He held up a small brown glass bottle. He walked over to a medical cabinet and returned with a syringe. He handed it to his daughter.

"This might hurt more than the cobra's fangs, but the result will feel better than my kisses." In her excitement, Mara didn't realize that her mother stood only a few feet away and overheard her. She blushed while rolling up Lawrence's sleeve and injected the serum.

"Ouch." Lawrence chuckled. "You'll have to kiss me again to make it feel better."

Mara saw her mother put her hands on her hips. She pursed her lips and nodded. Mara again kissed Lawrence's cheek. "Mother." She turned to Leena. "That was for therapy. I wanted to see if his fever has lessened."

"I'm glad at least that you've kept your sense of humor." Leena walked over to Lawrence. "You got the anti-venom and," she winked at her daughter, "tender loving care. You probably thought it couldn't get any better than that. I hope to prove you wrong. I think you're ready for solid food. Rest up. I am going to cook you curried fish. My husband caught it in the Brahmaputra."

"Thank you, ma'am," Lawrence smiled. "I can feel the anti-venom working already. I can't thank you enough."

"We're not the ones to thank, Mr. Mills." Leena smiled with tight lips. "Rest up. Dinner will be ready when you wake up. It may take a little longer because," she gazed at her daughter, who was holding Lawrence's hand, "I won't ask Mara to help me cook."

Mara released his hand. Leena half-smiled, held up her hand in a halt gesture, and nodded. Mara replied with a full smile, blushed, and again took Lawrence's hand.

***

The photographer, gaunt and pale from spending hours in the darkroom, stepped into Browning's parlor. Round spectacles magnified his eyes. With fingers yellowed by developer and tobacco, the photographer placed a finished photograph on the table. Nigel Browning picked it up and held it before his eyes. "Excellent! You have successfully caught the image of a goddess. You have earned a bonus. This photograph will serve me well." Browning pointed at his bearer, "Rahman. Pay Mr. Chatterjee his agreed-upon fee plus a ten-rupee bonus and show him to my carriage. Afterward, go to the telegraph room and have Cyril wire Calcutta. Summon Marco Bellini to my estate as soon as possible. Money is no object. Let him know that I have spared nothing to prepare his workshop. After Rahman and the photographer departed, Browning snapped his fingers. Two seconds later, came the jingling of ankle bells.

Layla and Anjali stood before Sir Nigel, trembling with their hands folded before them, tacitly knowing that their future lives hinged on his words.

"You have met the Goddess Kali. You will soon take your place among her chosen daughters who have shed shame and mercy alike. Her commands, whether for her pleasure or for havoc, shall be unquestioned and obeyed with zeal. As twin tongues of Kali, you shall help shape the World's destiny." He

90

folded his hands, "its destruction, and its renewal. You may kiss each other now, as a sign of your submission to the goddess."

***

"I've eaten fresh lobster trapped in Maine's frigid waters at Bookbinder's in Philadelphia and dipped it in melted butter from Amish country," Lawrence held up a forkful of fish, "but this tops them all."

"It's Rohu," Brian raised his chin and grinned, "You'll never catch one in either the Charles, Hudson, or Delaware rivers. You'll have to go fishing with me in the Brahmaputra if you want to catch one and enjoy a second serving."

"Are you sure you didn't catch it in the River of Gold from El Dorado?" Lawrence smiled at Leena. "But it's far more than the fish that made this meal splendid. All compliments to the chef. I can't thank you both enough."

"You're welcome." Leena nodded. "It was my pleasure."

"For dessert, I want to sing you something special." Mara stood and extended her hand. "I've practiced it, and I'm ready to share it with you."

Lawrence took her hand. She led him to the chapel.

Leena sighed. Brian smiled and squeezed his wife's hand. Leena took a deep breath, tensed her lips, and only slightly nodded.

***

"I know we said a prayer of thanksgiving for your health and healing before dinner. We need to pray again. Lawrence, the Lord works in mysterious ways. I confess that it troubles me to understand his ways in bringing good out of evil?"

"I don't understand, Mara."

91

"Sir Nigel gave us the anti-venom." Mara closed her eyes and bowed her head. "Lawrence, I know the blood of Jesus cleanses our spirits. We had to visit him in his manor to get it. The vileness of the man and his abode linger in my bones."

"That you and your family ventured into that snake pit on my behalf makes me appreciate you even more." Lawrence closed his eyes and shook his head. "The more I get to know Nigel Browning, the more I suspect that he teeters on the brink of madness. Yet his deception is intoxicating. He is a man of extreme intelligence and capability. His estate and successful operation speak for themselves. His stature and charisma make him even more convincing and dangerous."

"Yes. Lawrence. Although there is something in his aura that I find repellent, I cannot deny he is a handsome man, and the spirit that dwells within him is powerful."

"Mara, please take no offense to this. I am not in your country as a missionary. I am here to build a railroad. While I am under no obligation to convert to anyone's faith, my professional mission demands that I respect local customs. A Muslim minority works for me on the line. It's essential to the well-being of the operation that I let them break for their prayer ritual. I must also honor the practices of my Hindu workers. Yet Browning's beliefs are a perversion of any established order. Unfortunately, he does present them convincingly and temptingly."

"As a missionary's daughter, I fully understand the importance of understanding and respecting local traditions and customs, although I admit that I'm often confused about where my mixed blood and ancestry stand. A universal truth is that evil is cunning and self-serving, masking its hunger beneath the guise of desire. Lucifer was God's Angel of Light. Yet he hungered for more and convinced a third of the angels to join him in rebellion against God. He later promised Jesus all the world's kingdoms if he would worship him. Jesus replied, 'What profit a man to gain the entire world but to lose his soul?' Even wickedness will one day yield to God's command. The venom that threatened your life was born of the serpent, yet the cure was drawn from the same creature's fangs. How strange that even venom carries the seed of mercy. Perhaps the Lord allows evil to serve his ends, even when the hand that helps offers only harm."

"I think we can also thank Doctor Albert Calmette." Lawrence chuckled. "He invented the anti-venom in the first place."

"Yes, of course, Lawrence. All things work together for the good of those who love the Lord. The song I'm going to sing to you is an example of what we spoke about. God has the power to turn potential harm into good, and all things do work together for the good of those who love him. The hand of a man opposed to the God that I love and revere wrote the words to this song. I will sing it to you in German and then translate it for you."

Mara sat behind the Sutcliffes' piano and played the opening notes. A before a deep D trembled beneath her hand, opening for another, softer and even more mysterious melody that rose and fell like her heartbeat, A…G…F…G…C, until her voice entered, the beautiful, ethereal, and mysterious richness that was only Mara's…" O Mensche! Gib Acht! Was spricht die tiefe Mitternacht? Ich schlief, ich schlif- Aus tiefen Traum bin erwatch. Die Welt ist tief, Lust tiefer noch als Herzeleid: Weh spricht Vergeh! Doch alle Lust will Ewigkeit-will tiefe, tiefe Ewigkeit."

Lawrence was thunderstruck. The light of dusk caught her profile softly like candlelight flickering with a warm draft. It made him think, *Who is this Mara that Heaven should lend its voice to her lips? Lips I dare not kiss.*

Her final note dissolved, but the music lived on in her speaking voice as she half-sung, half-whispered, the German turning to English. "Oh man! Take heed! What says the deep midnight! I slept; I slept-from a deep dream have I awoken. The world is deep, deeper than day had thought. Deep in its woe, yet deeper still is joy than heartbreak. Woe says- Pass away! But all joy seeks eternity, seeks deep, deep eternity." Mara smiled. "Lawrence, you see the World's reason but not yet its meaning."

"Yes, we live at the peak of enlightenment and two centuries of great thinkers from Schopenhauer to Schiller, to Darwin and Freud. All of them make sense in their own way. Schopenhauer was a pessimist who considered suffering an intrinsic part of existence. I prefer Schiller's appreciation of beauty and freedom through art. Darwin and Freud expounded the rational and scientific but failed to bridge the spiritual."

"Yes, Lawrence, I can tell you seek that bridge from the rational to the spiritual, and you're considering God's ultimate triumph over evil. Gustav Mahler put those words from Friedrich Nietzsche's novel, Thus Spoke Zarathustra, into music. It was the fourth movement of his third symphony."

"But Nietzsche declared God is dead."

"Yes. He did. But his words were lament rather than triumph. Nietzsche wrote of man reaching for something beyond himself, yet he reached into the void and found nothing. Mahler was raised in the old faith and endured harsh sorrows. He sought the same height and found it in Christ. The final movements of his Third Symphony sing of man's renewal through faith in God. I have read the sheet music while following along with a scratchy record played on a gramophone at the Gauhati library. Nellie Melba sang the fourth movement. The gramophone horn made her voice sound even more distant, yet her voice reached into my soul. I long to one day hear her sing in person and hear an orchestra perform the symphony."

Lawrence took both of Mara's hands. "I just heard in person a singer every bit as great as the Australian soprano."

She's an inspiration, and if I practice hard, maybe someday," Mara closed her eyes, "but I am not now in her class."

"That's a matter of opinion, and I have attended opera in New York and Philadelphia. Mara, I need to confess something."

"I am here for you, Lawrence."

"You have opened my eyes about Sir Nigel's offer to follow him. It is seductive and tempting. It offers all the world's pleasures and even immortality by becoming a God. He claims I will rule with him and the Goddess Kali, but you made me realize that I would only be serving him, myself, and a lie."

"Jesus offers something beyond anything this world has to offer. Satan thought he could end Jesus's message by provoking man's evil to kill him on the cross. Yet Jesus defeated both evil and death. He rose from the dead and gave us eternal life as his gift of sacrifice and love. His blood will not make you a God, but you will live eternally with him as a child of God."

"What Browning proposes borders on madness. That our Friedrich Nietzsche died in madness serves as my warning. You touch on what Browning's offer lacks. Paul tells us in Thessalonians that all is vanity unless done with love. Mara," Lawrence squeezed her hands and looked deep into her luminous brown eyes. "Everything you have done for me, every word you have spoken, has solved history's greatest mystery. Love. Oh, Mara, I have come to a decision. I want to pray with you in God's presence. Lawrence and Mara held hands and bowed their heads. 'Lord Jesus, I have heard your word before, but I chose not to listen. Now your spirit speaks, and I choose to obey. I do believe that you died for me and rose again. Forgive me and take me as I am. Cleanse my spirit with your blood and come into my heart, be my Lord and Savior. Let me live my days on Earth and eternally in Heaven as your servant. Amen."

"Amen." Tears welled in Mara's eyes.

Invigorated yet weightless, euphoric yet sober, Lawrence saw light glistening in Mara's tears.

They embraced.

Oh Lord, is it right to feel such joy in holding this man close to me? Mara held him tighter.

Lawrence touched his cheek to hers. Her hair brushed his cheek, soft as dawn's first whisper. Her aroma stirred a memory of the faint sweetness of a newborn. Mara's closeness reached past his physical senses, transporting him into a realm of tranquility. *No. No. Honor and care for this precious child of God.* Lawrence pulled away. Yet their hands remained clasped; their heads moved slowly towards each other. Their lips met. Briefly. Just a dry peck. But still a kiss. "You saved my mortal life, Mara. For that, I will be grateful forever. And now I know Jesus will never let me go. He has saved my immortal soul. I will be grateful to you forever."

"Jesus always loved you, Lawrence." Mara took a deep breath before smiling. "Now he can love you for eternity."

Galloping hooves broke their reverie. Corporal Stanton rushed into the chapel. "Lawrence! You're up and about. Thank God. This just arrived from the British military infirmary in Calcutta. Cobra anti-venom!"

"Thanks to her," Lawrence nodded at Mara. "I already received a dose."

"Just one dose? Sir, again, you underestimate the jungle's power. A cobra's venom is nothing to be trifled with. You can relapse at any moment and even perish."

"The Corporal is right, Lawrence. Let's thank God's providence and the British Army." Mara walked over to the Corporal and took the glass vial from him. "I thank you from the bottom of my heart." She filled a syringe with the serum and injected it into Lawrence's arm.

How I want to, but I know I can't, Lawrence thought as she massaged the injection site.

Chapter 13

Rather than shield his eyes from the rising sun, Lawrence admired its golden glow on the Brahmaputra River. Its normally muddy water was clear this morning, tempting Lawrence to scan the surface for a rohu. He looked up from the river and spotted an Amur falcon. "Soar high, my feathered friend. May you also find Heaven." *Many things I never dreamed would happen have happened. Not the least of which is being back on the job and being happy about it.* The native workers' machetes flashing and flailing against bamboo and bracken struck a chord like a military drumroll. A sudden stillness fell over the site, a silence as rigid as its British Army security detail. Lawrence failed to notice the approaching horses.

"You should be dead, Mr. Mills." Sir Nigel, wearing his tailored white linen Edwardian riding attire, sat on his prize stallion. Rahman and two other bodyguards and bearers, Katara daggers at their sides, sat on their horses behind him. "Thanks to me, you're alive. Your destiny as Shiva's son Skanda would not permit me to let you die."

"I do owe you gratitude for supplying the anti-venom."

"Gratitude is too feeble a currency for the value of your life, Mr. Mills. You do know that cobra anti-venom is worth fifty times more than its weight in gold. Moreover, it's as rare as mercy from Kali." Browning slid higher on his horse and pointed at Lawrence, "And you received both. Deadly snakes are common in India. Viper and Cobra strikes are a known hazard for my plantation workers. Snake bite means that they die in place. Later, the vultures pick their flesh, and their bones nourish my fields. Only one thing matters: advancing Kali's mission of destruction and renewal. When the goddess rises, and I marry her as Shiva, and we adopt you as Skanda, you will fully understand. At that time, you will learn how to wield power and not just over the duties and wages of workers, but the power of life and death. The cobra lacks that power. Possessing anti-venom gives me that power. You have passed your first lesson. On the day that Kali rises, the cobras and vipers will obey our commands. Their fangs and venom will be weapons against our enemies. This Saturday night, I summon you to my Temple of Kali so that I may anoint you as Skanda to our followers. Her order is secret. The identity of her followers will shock you. That will be revealed to you on Saturday."

"Sir Nigel, I am flattered by your offer. You are an impressive man, and I admit that I found your offer tempting. I gave it considerable thought. Nevertheless, I have decided to follow the King of Kings. Jesus Christ."

"Ha! Ha! Ha! King of Kings? You are a rational man, Mr. Mills. Is there any proof behind the church's claims? Or are they as deceitful, greedy, and self-serving as non-believers? We live in the twentieth century, not the Middle Ages. You are of European descent, not a dusky jungle savage. Science and rationality have overcome superstition and fantasy. Darwin has proven that life and humans have evolved. You and I know that it's only by Kali's hand. Instead of Christianity, why not convert to Islam, Buddhism, Judaism, or an unenlightened sect of Hinduism? All are the same. All will kneel and bow to their non-existent Gods. I am Shiva. I stand before you with a power and glory that will blossom to unimaginable heights when Kali rises. As our son Skanda, you will never bow or kneel to anyone. Feel the power that you now command. The workers and even British soldiers must obey you without question. Now imagine nations kneeling and bowing in obedience to you. You are almost ready. Saturday night, Mr. Mills."

"Satan already made that offer to Jesus. You put a price on a man's life. How about the value of his immortal soul?"

"Did I not tell you that once Kali anoints you as her son, Skanda, you will achieve immortality as a God? Satan and Jesus do not exist. Your God is an invention of an ancient nomadic tribe. Later, belief in his supposed son was perfected by a Roman Caesar to consolidate his power. You now see reality before your very eyes. I bow to no one. Kali and I will be equal partners as husband and wife. Do not bow to a false God. Have the nations bow to you as a real God. Skanda."

"Paul says in Philippians, 'In the name of Jesus every knee shall bow, of all things in Heaven, and all things in Earth, and all things under the Earth. Every tongue shall confess that Jesus is Lord, and to the glory of God the Father.' That includes you, Sir Nigel."

"I see that Sunday school taught you well. You think, as Kali's mate, I don't know the Bible, the Quran, the Talmud, and the Hindu Vedas?" Sir Nigel raised his palms and pointed his fingertips at Lawrence. "I give you credit for your courage, Mr. Mills. No man has ever spoken to me with such disrespect and gone unpunished. Again, that gives me reason to choose you over men of much higher standing. Look around you, Mr. Mills. You didn't break your workers, yet they stand motionless in my presence. I will give you until Saturday to come to your senses and join me in Kali's Temple. Good day, Mr. Mills." Sir Nigel led his horse-mounted entourage away in a four-beat trot.

***

A thin Assamese boy dressed in white ran up to Corporal Stanton and handed him a small silver cylinder. He removed a note and read it; afterwards, the Corporal stuffed it in his pocket, handed the cylinder back to the boy, and rode over to Lawrence. "Lawrence, I got a message from my superiors. You are aware that anti-venom is a precious and expensive commodity. The British military is sending a nurse to conduct a follow-up exam on you. They need a written report, both to justify its usage and its efficacy. She wants to meet us this afternoon at the Dak Bungalow. I'm sure the American missionary will allow the use of his clinic. Please, allow me to accompany you."

"I can deal with it myself. No need for you to do extra duty on my behalf."

"I don't think you understand, sir." Corporal Stanton relaxed his posture and grinned sheepishly. "You are here as an American civilian. A British soldier must obey regulations. Unlike you, I am prohibited from courting local women. Nurse Fairleigh, Amanda is her first name, is a proper Englishwoman. She's part of Queen Alexandra's Imperial Military Nursing Service. Before we joined up and volunteered for India, I met her once at the Deptford and Bermondsey library. She even agreed to meet me for a cup of tea afterwards. She can make even an undertaker smile. I swear she's got sunshine bottled up inside her. I surely will never forget her. I just hope she remembers me. She doesn't look as ravishing as Mara, but I fancy her just the same."

"Now that you put it that way." Lawrence slapped Douglas's arm. "Of course, you can accompany me."

***

"There she is," Corporal Stanton pointed at Nurse Fairleigh. She stood several inches shorter than Douglas or Lawrence. Her gray uniform, white cuffs and collar, as well as her linen apron and scarlet belt, fit well over her ten extra pounds. A folded cap with a red cross emblem topped her friendly, round face. A pair of round-framed eyeglasses sat on her button nose. "She smiled!" Douglas tapped Lawrence's arm. "I hope it was for me."

"Good afternoon, Corporal Stanton." Nurse Fairleigh twinkled her eyes. "Or may I call you Douglas?"

"You remembered!" Corporal Stanton beamed.

"How can I forget? It's not every stranger I meet in a library that I later agree to share tea with. Did you bring our patient? It can't be him." She gazed at Lawrence. "He looks as healthy as the king's own, or shall I say," she chuckled, "the president's own?"

"He received two doses of anti-venom." Corporal Stanton dismounted his horse and secured it to a post. "One from a private source and one from the king."

"I'd like to know how you survived until you got the anti-venom." Nurse Fairleigh adjusted her cap. "A cobra bite is usually fatal unless anti-venom is administered post haste."

Lawrence had also dismounted and secured his horse.

Corporal Stanton spoke before Lawrence could answer. "You will soon meet the reason why. She is self-taught. Her father is a Baptist missionary from the United States, and her mother is Assamese. She doubles as a schoolteacher and a nurse at the missionary dispensary. To see her is never to forget her." Douglas winced. "That didn't come out right. After all, even though the two of us only met once and we only exchanged one letter since we came to India as part of the King's military, I surely hadn't forgotten you."

"I understand," Nurse Fairleigh chuckled. "Don't worry, I'm too busy with my QAIMNS duties to waste time in front of a mirror."

"Well, I surely appreciate you providing a dose of anti-venom." Lawrence smiled and nodded to the nurse. "It put me over the top. I understand why you need to do a follow-up exam. Cooperating is the least I can do."

"I'm sure you've worked with my countrymen enough to know that we're all about regulations, procedures, and paperwork." The corner of her mouth tightened into a knowing smile. "If it isn't recorded, it hasn't happened."

"Mara is the woman I told you about who kept him alive." Douglas looked at Lawrence with a sly smile. "I'm sure she won't mind us using her clinic for your exam. Come. It's close enough for us to walk."

***

Mara stood before her last class. "Who can give me a sentence using a verb of being and a complement?" Mara chuckled. "That's complement with an 'e' as in complete, not an 'I' as in praise. If any of you were thinking about answering, "The bumblebee made a pretty hive, you're incorrect."

The class laughed.

"Okay, Padma," Mara pointed to a young girl. "Would you like to try?"

"Yes, Miss Sutcliffe, "The queen bee was happy with her hive."

"Excellent. The queen bee is your noun subject. 'Was' is a verb of being and serves as a linking verb. 'Happy with her hive' is an adjective phrase functioning as a subject complement." Mara looked up. "I can see by the beat of our clock that our time is up. For homework…"

The class groaned.

"…Write ten sentences with a verb of being and a complement." Mara left with her class and watched them walk away in different directions. She beamed at the sight of Lawrence, Corporal Stanton, and a QAIMNS nurse approaching. As if angel wings sprouted from her shoes, Mara ran up to them. "Lawrence!" *Should I hug him? Better not in front of Corporal Stanton and this British nurse.*

"Nurse Fairleigh," Douglas' eyes widened while smiling at Mara, "I proudly introduce you to Mara, the one who saved the American engineer's life."

"Well, Douglas," Nurse Fairleigh glanced at the Corporal before walking to Mara and holding both of her hands. "I excuse you for saying that no one could forget her. If I possessed such beauty, I daresay I could heal patients just by looking at them."

Mara closed her eyes, blushed, and lowered her head.

"I beg your pardon, Miss Mara." Nurse Fairleigh released Mara's hands. "That came out all wrong."

"At least it came from a lady." Douglas smiled at the nurse. "A gentleman could never make such a remark."

"Nurse Fairleigh," Lawrence added, "her home has more books than the American Library of Congress. I am alive today because of her knowledge."

"Don't leave out the power of God." Mara raised her head and smiled.

"Of course," Nurse Fairleigh smiled. "It took living thousands of miles from home and surrounded by multiple religions before truly finding Jesus. Well, the British are notorious for their formality. We have an American, a beautiful woman with an Assamese mother, and Corporal Stanton, whom I am already acquainted with, and whom I already know by first name. Therefore, you can all call me Amanda."

"And you can drop the Miss." Mara smiled. "My last name is Sutcliffe, but please call me Mara."

"Well, Mara, you probably have more medical knowledge than I do. Nevertheless, as you are aware, cobra anti-venom is rare and costly. It's just a formality, but the British higher-ups want some paperwork justifying its usage and, seeing that it's a recent discovery, its effectiveness."

***

Lawrence rolled up his sleeve and sat on the examination table in the Sutcliffes' dispensary. Amanda measured his pulse. Yet Mara made Lawrence's heartbeat gallop like the hooves of a racehorse as their glances met and lingered before either could look away. Amanda wrote in her medical log. "Your pulse is abnormally fast." She chuckled. "But I can tell it's not because of cobra venom or anti-venom." She winked. "I'll adjust my findings to make my superiors happy. The QAIMNS has put me up in the Dak Bungalow for the night, and they gave me meal vouchers. Why don't the four of us go? Mara, I understand your position as a missionary's daughter and your dual duties as a schoolteacher and a nurse. Seeing that both Douglas and I are in uniform, the four of us walking together won't provoke any gossip."

"Mara?" Lawrence held her hand. "What do you say?" Mara glanced at Douglas and then Amanda. She met Lawrence's gaze and saw it in a softened light, the look of a man both reverent and undone.

Even though she was aware of Amanda and Douglas, Mara did not withdraw her hand. Looking only at Lawrence, she said, "Yes."

***

Lawrence and Mara walked over to a table in the Dak Bungalow's main dining room. "Oh no, you don't." Amanda laughed, doffed her cap, and pulled her hairpin. Ash blonde hair cascaded to her shoulders. "I'm finding us a table far removed from prying eyes." She took Douglas's hand and led him to a private room.

Lawrence looked at Mara and nodded his head in their direction. She followed him without holding his hand, yet trembling passed through her heart to her feet as she walked a step behind him. They sat at a corner table. Amanda took off her eyeglasses, folded them, and placed them on the table. "I don't need glasses to see that I'm seated with two handsome men," she chuckled, "And a woman as beautiful and mysterious as the one in that painting." Amanda pointed to a print of John William Waterhouse's *The Lady of Shalot* hanging on the wall behind their table. Mara looked up and pondered the painting of a red-haired woman adrift in a boat with three candles flickering between her face and the dark water. The image struck her as both a warning

104

and a forbidden prayer. She turned from the print to Lawrence. She noticed the lamplight glancing across his cheek and jaw. *The light is steady, but my heartbeat won't stay still. His mouth is so enticing. It's moving in a half-formed thought. What does he want to say to me? Why do I flutter so? What is pulling me toward him?* She lifted her right hand, wanting to touch his cheek. *'No.'* Mara folded her hands.

"I'm paying for this with vouchers, Douglas." Amanda broke Mara's reverie. "But I'd never rob a man of his proper duty." Amanda held Douglas's hand. "Go on, be gallant, fetch the wine."

Mara tried to speak, whatever bound her heart to her voice had fallen silent. Lawrence reached out and grasped her right hand. She unfolded her hands and let him pull her right hand toward him. She neither squeezed it nor pulled it away.

Douglas returned with a dusty, green bottle of wine in a wire mesh. "Viola." He held four glasses by the stem and placed them on the table. After pulling the cork from the bottle with a corkscrew, he poured burgundy wine into their glasses. He held up his glass. "To Lawrence, and our intrepid nurses, Amanda and Mara, for saving his life."

The four tapped glasses. Mara stared at her wine glass.

"I doubt that vintage is 1900 years old and turned into wine from water." Amanda giggled. "Nevertheless, Mara, it's no sin to enjoy a sip." Amanda disarmed Mara with a wide smile.

Mara turned to Lawrence. He grinned and nodded. The four drank together. "Mara, Lawrence, will you please excuse Douglas and me? We wish to venture to the balcony and view the sunset."

"But, I…" Douglas spread his hands.

Amanda pursed her lips, grabbed Douglas's hand, and pulled him to his feet.

Douglas grinned and nodded to Amanda. He muttered without moving his lips, "I get it." They walked hand in hand from the private dining room.

Lawrence and Mara remained. They continued to hold hands. "Lawrence, you've seen the world. I have a brother living in America. He's written letters about your country, and my father has told me many things about your land." She blushed. "But I've seldom left this village. We visited my mother's family in Calcutta once when I was a child, and we recently went to Guahati. I am grateful for my parents and having many books. My mother and father taught me foreign languages, musical craft, voice, and piano; also, scripture, medicine, and more. Yet many mysteries remain. I love my parents, and they love me. I understand that. God loves us most of all. It's no mystery that his love for us is beyond comprehension. After all, he came to Earth as a man, suffered a horrible death on the cross as payment for our sins, and gave us eternal life. Scripture tells us that love is patient and kind. It rejoices in truth and endures all things. Love is not boastful, proud, jealous, rude, self-seeking, easily angered, or resentful. Yet a mystery remains beyond my understanding." She held his hand and looked deeply into his eyes, "Lawrence, may I ask you something?"

"Please do, Mara." He moved his head closer to her. "Anything at all."

"When you were delirious from the cobra venom. You shouted the name, Dorothy. Who was Dorothy?"

"Dorothy is why we are sitting here together. We were engaged to be married. Her father tricked me into taking this position to get me away from her."

"Why would he not approve of you? I believe you're a man of high character- the highest- and I can tell that my parents agree. My mother is wary, but I know deep inside, she sees you in the same light as I. But why didn't Dorothy's parents feel the same?"

"You, as an Assamese, will have no trouble understanding. I'm sure your father told you that the United States does not have a caste system like India or England. Nevertheless, Dorothy's family, the Cabots, were of much higher socio-economic standing than my family."

"I am only a missionary's daughter. We live by humble means. Would the Mills's approve?"

"Mara, your parents are intelligent, educated, and wise. They could hold an in-depth conversation with my parents. They would know that your parents could've gotten rich and risen high in American society. Yet your parents chose to serve something higher than themselves. That shows a character lacking in many social circles. So, don't worry about my parents; they possess something George and Diana Cabot lack. A heart. They will respect any choice that I make."

"This Dorothy Cabot. Did you love her?"

Lawrence took a deep breath. "Yes, Mara. I loved her."

"How did you know that you loved her?"

"Well, Mara, every time I was near her, I felt drawn to her, like the gravity that holds us to God's Earth. Sometimes her presence gave me a tingling, light-headed euphoria, like after drinking a first glass of wine. At other times, her presence gave me a surge of energy, like a first cup of strong, morning coffee. When I was away from her, I felt like those cups were drained. Building a future with her inspired me to work harder."

"Do you still love her?"

"No, Mara." Lawrence took a deep breath. "During the time we were together, I confess that I was sometimes jealous of other men. I also took boastful pride in being seen with her on my arm. After it ended, I had to wrestle with the demon of anger and bitterness because of her and her father's betrayal." Lawrence tapped her hand. "You didn't have to tell me what Paul wrote to the Corinthians about love: you have shown me. Your leading me to Jesus and the way to forgiveness was more than mere words. You glowed with his love. Now Jesus has given me peace in my heart. I no longer love or hate Dorothy. I wish her well and hope she finds what she and her family seek."

"I never met Dorothy. I also forgive her and her family for hurting you." Mara winced and dropped her head. "Now I ask that you forgive me. I admit." She closed her eyes and lowered her head. "I am a bit jealous of Dorothy. If she could win the love of a man like you, she must be even more beautiful than the woman in the painting. I am also guilty of selfishness. I am grateful to Dorothy's parents. Without their shenanigans, you would not be here with me. Lawrence. You have solved a mystery for me. The emotional tingling, light-headedness, or energy surge that you describe…When we are together, my cup runneth over. When we're apart, it's empty. You inspire me to do better work for my Lord. Lawrence," she squeezed his hand and looked deep into his eyes. "Only Jesus was perfect. Maybe you were sometimes jealous and prideful. Yet I know Dorothy filled your heart with much loveliness. Lawrence, I feel those things for you. Lawrence, I love you."

"Mara," Lawrence looked at her. *Her radiant glow. How can anything beneath Heaven be so beautiful?* "I love you too."

"Lawrence, I will always love God above all. The other day, when our lips met, I now know I made a mistake."

"What do you mean?" Lawrence took her hands and softly gazed into her eyes. "There's nothing wrong with sharing a peck on the lips."

Mara squeezed his hands in return and moved her head closer. "You don't understand my mistake." Mara kissed Lawrence on the lips, her tongue mingling with his. *A childhood memory of running up a hill surged through her. At the top, she danced, gazing out at the world below. She spread her arms wide and let the wind catch her dress. Her joyful laughter sang to the heavens.* Mara put her hands behind his head and dug her fingers into his hair. She would not let him pull away.

Chapter 14

Lawrence sat astride his horse. He leaned forward and spoke to him. "If you felt like how I feel this morning, you could sprout wings and fly like Pegasus. Well, my four-legged friend, what would Sigmund Freud have to say about a man speaking to a horse, and a gelding at that, about his love for a woman?" A faint rainbow shimmered in the morning mist, and at its end, he pictured Mara's visage. "The workers' pounding, chopping, and digging never change," he unfolded his map. *We have two weeks of relatively easy terrain before the hills. I want to sit here and dream of her, but I remember what I said about her inspiring me. The railroad will improve the lives of her people. I should mind my work.*

***

Mara's school day ended. After waving goodbye to her pupils as they dispersed, she walked over to the clinic, sat in a chair, folded her hands, and prayed, "Heavenly Father, in the name of Jesus, I pray that you forgive my sins, including the ones that I am unsure of. Elation fills my soul, Lord Jesus. Can this feeling be wrong, Lord? I know you never meant for me to be alone, and you blessed Adam and Eve and told them to be fruitful and multiply. Lord, keep me strong until the day I can lawfully fulfill my love for Lawrence and follow your will. Please, keep Lawrence close to you and protect him. In the name of the Father, Son, and Holy Ghost. Amen."

A little boy ran into the clinic crying. "Miss Mara! I fell. I hurt my knee. Please make it better, Miss Mara. It hurts."

"Aww…Rupen…You poor thing. Have a seat," Mara patted the examining table. "Let me make it better."

The boy sat on the examining table.

"It's just a little scrape. First, let's clean it up." Mara wiped dust from the boy's knee with a wet rag. "You're already being so brave, my precious little Rupen." She dipped a swab into amber iodine. "Now I need you to be even braver. This is going to sting a little. But it will be over before you can say, Jack Robinson. As soon as I put this medicine on your knee, say, Jack Robinson."

"Ouch…Jack Robinson."

Mara blanched. A sickness worse than any she had ever treated coursed through her veins. She lifted her eyes to the dispensary entrance. Sir Nigel stood there, his gaze cutting straight to her soul.

I behold the Goddess. Courtesy forbids a gentleman to stare. Yet courtesy binds only mortal men. She has roused Shiva's power within me. She is no mortal woman. She is Kali. From my eyes, may Shiva's divine power flow into her and awaken the goddess Kali that slumbers inside her.' Browning's body remained rigid: his expression stoic and his gaze steadfast.

Mara grabbed the boy's hand and pulled him from the table. "Come with me, Rupen. Don't ask why. Just come with me." Mara led him to a supply closet. She took him inside and locked the door.

I will not pursue her as a common man besotted with a mortal woman. Let her remain fearful. Machiavelli wrote, It is better to be feared than loved, if you cannot be both. Our day will come. Divine destiny will unite us. Together, we shall destroy and renew the world in our image.

***

Nigel Browning walked into the Sutcliffe residence without knocking. Rahman, Katara dagger at his side, stood in the doorway.

Brian Sutcliffe sat with Leena on a couch. Leena blanched and covered her heaving heartbeat with her hands. Brian stood and

110

pointed. "Just because you're the richest and most powerful man in Assam doesn't give you the right to barge into my home."

Sir Nigel held up his hand in a halt gesture. "Relax, Mr. Sutcliffe. This is not a courtesy call. What I have to offer will make you wealthy enough to replace this hovel with a palace." Browning sat in one of the Sutcliffe's chairs.

"Firstly, this hovel, as you call it, is a home. A palace without love is no home." Brian jutted his jaw. "It's no more than an expensive inn with empty rooms." Brian sat. Leena clung to him.

"Mrs. Sutcliffe, you will understand my proposal better than your husband. Courtship is the custom of modern America and England. In a more civilized age, marriages were arranged to unite fortunes and further power. Love, in time, found its place."

"Your point, Sir Nigel?" Rev Sutcliffe tilted his head.

"I can do more than make you rich. I can give your daughter a better life than you could ever pray for."

"So, you know my prayers? My calling is to bring Jesus to men like you." Brian pointed at Nigel. "Until that happens, don't tell me what I pray for."

"I see. Pride. Every man has his price, Reverend Sutcliffe. I expected yours to be higher than most. I am here to offer you a princely dowry for your daughter's hand in marriage. Need I say that I can give her a far better life than what you or your God has ever provided?"

"Again, you mistake my faith for poverty, Sir Nigel." Reverend Sutcliffe stood, arms flared. "And only a man with deluded arrogance such as yours would think my daughter is for sale. The God you mock has given her more than your wealth could ever buy- a pure heart, a sound mind, and the will to choose to follow God and to marry the man that he chooses for her."

Browning laughed. "You speak of delusion, yet you worship it. What is a woman if not a man's rightful possession? Tell me,

Reverend. What reward lies in seeing her wed to a man of common means? Or worse, she ends up a lonely old spinster doomed to death without leaving you descendants. Stifle your pride, Reverend, and do what's right for your daughter."

"If you have come to tempt my wife or me, you waste your time. I will pray that God Himself will shield my daughter's eyes from the darkness in yours. I would say that you are no longer welcome here, but you were never welcome in the first place." Brian Sutcliffe prodded. "Now leave and take your thug with you."

"No man who disrespects me goes unpunished, Reverend Sutcliffe. I am placing before you an offer that only a fool would refuse." Browning put an envelope on the table. "Read the fine print, Reverend Sutcliffe. I am a man of patience, but my patience is not unlimited. You have until Sunday afternoon to accept my offer. My offer includes overlooking your insolence. "Good day," he paused for effect, "Reverend." He bowed to Leena. "And good day to you, Mrs. Sutcliffe." I can see where your daughter inherited her beauty."

***

Lawrence nodded to the Sirdar, signaling that work was done for the day. The Sirdar blew a long blast into his Pepa horn. The workers put their tools in a pile and dispersed. Lawrence gazed at the setting sun. He imagined Mara's smiling face replacing its golden glow. *Thursday is in the books. That's one day down and just two to go until I see her again. Will she greet me with a kiss and say that she loves me? Will she say it over and over again, just as my mind keeps repeating, I love you, Mara. I love you. I love you, over and over again.* He rode his horse on a riding trail toward his quarters. Two riders appeared from the shadows.

Sir Nigel, Rahman by his side, stopped in front of him. "It's Thursday night, Mr. Mills. I cannot yet address you as Skanda.

One way or another, in forty-eight hours, you will be either a God or a sacrifice to the Goddess. You claim Jesus gives you a choice. I'm doing the same."

Lawrence leaned back a fraction, his shoulders hunched. He averted his eyes from Browning. His nerves tingled until his muscles threatened to give way.

"Good evening, Mr. Mills." Browning tipped his pith helmet. "Until Saturday." Browning and Rahman galloped away into the gloaming.

Coward. The thought haunted him. He closed his eyes and steepled his hands, *Dear Lord, forgive my weakness. Why do I fear a man when you promise that if you are for us, no one can be against us?* Lawrence bowed his head. *Peter denied you three times, and later, you entrusted him with the keys to the kingdom of God. Paul wrote that we are up against the powers of darkness. Browning is a formidable and dark foe. Give me strength, Lord; give me strength.*

***

Mara opened the closet door. "Come, Rupen. The danger is over."

"But I'm scared, Miss Mara."

"I was also afraid. A terrible man was watching us. Your parents warned you that bad men are out there. I will protect you; your parents will protect you; and God will protect you." Mara smiled at the boy. "Now let's finish fixing your knee." She took gauze and medical tape from a shelf in the closet.

"Thank you, Miss Mara." Rupen smiled. "It doesn't hurt anymore."

***

113

Mara stepped inside her home. Her parents sat motionless. Their faces looked as if they were dredged in white flour. "Mother, Father, I saw Sir Nigel. I take it he's been here."

"Please sit with us, Mara." Leena pointed at a chair. "Yes. He was here. We are terrified like you. If ever Satan Himself walked the Earth as a man, it's Sir Nigel."

"Mara, our faith will now be tested as never before, and I hope never again." Brian held up his hands.

"We discussed sending you to Calcutta to live with your grandparents." Leena pursed her lips. "But you would still not escape Browning's reach."

"I am considering resigning from my post and bringing us all to the United States. After all, your brother is already there."

"Father, I have often dreamed of America. Just as you have come to India in the service of the Lord, I am serving the Lord here as well. Our people need me. The children need me. When it's the Lord's timing, I hope to live in the United States. Yet we can't flee and abandon our ministry because we're afraid of a man."

"You're right, Mara. We will follow the lead of the Apostles and continue our ministry in courage and in truth." Brian took Leena's hand. Mara joined the link. He prayed, "Dear Heavenly Father, in the name of Jesus, we come before you as your humble servants. We face grave danger, but help us fear not, as our battle is not against man. If it be your will that we endure persecution, may the Holy Ghost fill us with the courage to endure to the end. Amen."

"Amen." Mara and Leena chimed in.

Chapter 15

Sir Nigel stood by a picture window overlooking his sprawling tea fields. The sight of horse-mounted overseers ensuring that the workers hacked and collected leaves into their wicker baskets failed to break his obsession. A house servant walked up to him. He stood still until his master acknowledged him. "Sir," he folded his hands in front of him and bowed, "Mr. Bellini. He says he's finished. He wants you to come to his workshop."

***

Marco Bellini greeted Nigel Browning with a wide smile. His gray smock was caked in paint, gypsum plaster, and jute.

He's smiling at me. Most men cringe in fear at my presence. "Mr. Bellini. I am informed that you have completed your commission."

"Yes, sir! May I unveil it?"

"Please do."

Marco Bellini strode over to the shrouded figure, its human contours faint beneath the canvas. He clutched the cover and smiled even wider. "Ecco!" He unsheathed his masterpiece.

Browning was stunned as if a bolt of blue shot him. His eyes seemed to have grown and escaped the confines of his skull. After ten seconds, he spoke. "You have created a living, breathing masterpiece." Browning raised his hands. "You not only came to me highly recommended, but I also hired you for one of the reasons that you left Florence. Your worship of beauty offended Rome. Here, beauty will worship you. Come to my parlor, Mr. Bellini. I wish to discuss an offer well beyond our agreed-upon fee."

***

"Tell me, Mr. Bellini." Sir Nigel sat upright. He steepled his fingers. "What was your life like in Florence?"

"I lived a simple life. Italy has many sculptors and too few patrons. The church gave me my big break. They commissioned me to sculpt the Virgin. She was to live in the Basilica of Santa Croce in Florence. I didn't want to sculpt just another statue. I aimed at capturing the divine feminine. After all, Beauty is Godliness. God's highest art is a beautiful woman, and therefore, the Holy Mother of God should reign as most beautiful of all. Beauty separates us from the beasts of the field. Beauty inspires us to reach for something higher than ourselves. My creation of the Virgin was meant to capture both her divinity and humanity as a woman and strengthen both faith and desire for God." He held up his hands.

"Did you succeed?"

"Well, Sir," Bellini squirmed in his chair. "I most surely did." He smiled. "At least in my eyes. In the eyes of the church, she was a blasphemy. They rejected my statue and refused to pay me. Moreover, my reputation was tarnished. As word spread, the patrons started to vanish. I finally sold her to an Englishman for enough to cover my fare to Calcutta. Rome seeks God and saints in cathedrals. Perhaps in India, I can find him in form and shadow."

"You came to find the divine in art, and you shall. Your church taught you that your God created Adam and Eve, and they were to be fruitful and multiply. Yet they were doomed to only multiply as humans and never evolve into Gods. The church rejected your genius because you dared to create the divine feminine. Kali, not a chaste virgin, is the divine feminine. Through her marriage to Shiva, the world will be destroyed and then renewed. Kali has the power to anoint a mortal and raise him among the Gods. I can see by your expression that my words have given you pause. Your church permits drinking wine, doesn't it?"

"Yes. It does."

"I'm sure Barolo of 1899 vintage will please you." Browning snapped his fingers twice. The next sound was the jingling of ankle bells. Anjali and Layla emerged barefoot in flowing silks that parted as they walked, revealing the grace of their legs in the lamplight. They wore silk wraps loosely over their breasts. Their abdomens were bare, lean, and smooth. Lilac perfume flavored their skin while hibiscus flowers adorned their fluffed, wavy hair. Anjali placed two wine glasses on the table. Layla poured from the bottle. "Salute."

Sir Nigel held up his glass of wine. Marco Bellini held his aloft and tapped his host's glass. Nigel placed his glass on the table and snapped his fingers. Anjali and Layla moved behind Marco and pressed their bodies to his. They massaged his shoulders before moving to his chest.

Bellini breathed in gasps. A bead of sweat emerged on his cheek. He chugged his entire glass of wine. Browning re-filled his glass.

"No need to resist their many charms, Mr. Bellini. Tell me. How are your quarters in Calcutta?"

"It's a pesthole."

"Your old religion does not appreciate the genius of your art. Rome shunned you for capturing the divine feminine. Moreover, the church, in its piety, would forbid you the heavenly pleasure of women, as if beauty itself were an offense. I shall give you a revelation. Shiva lives within me. When I am united with Kali, Shiva will be released, and I shall rise with her as a God. Join us, and you too will become a God. You shall be our divine artist.

Kali will lavishly reward every image you create. The nations will fall to their knees in worship and adoration to each one. I am aware of Calcutta's slums. I have a brick, plastered, and whitewashed guest house with a wrap-around veranda ready for you. It has a bedroom, parlor, kitchen, and dining room. Servants will clean and cook for you. After all, mundane chores are for mortals. Do you acknowledge me as divine, and do you accept my offer?"

Anjali wrapped her arm across Bellini's chest. Layla clasped his right hand. Marco breathed deeply through his nose and licked his lips.

"Once you have tasted my reward of Kali's daughters, there is no turning back. Through them the Goddess breathes, and through me she acts. Layla, Anjali, show our disciple to his home. He has crossed the threshold of the divine."

Layla pulled Bellini to his feet. Anjali took his other hand. Together, they led him toward his new home. Desire had snared and bound him like a spider's silk; his reason ebbed with each step.

Chapter 16

Sunday. The morning mist dripped from the leaves, bracken, and fronds like teardrops. Lawrence and Corporal Stanton rode together on horseback en route to Sundarpur. "What's with the silence this morning. What's the matter? Cat got your tongue?"

"I wouldn't call it a cat." Lawrence put his reins to his side. "More like a dragon."

"Let me guess. Sir Nigel"

"Yes, Douglas, earlier in the week, he insisted I join him in his madness by participating in his ceremony. He held it last night. If I were a soldier at wartime, I imagine you might have had me tied to a post and shot for cowardice. I took the easy way out and told him I would attend. Just as Peter denied Jesus three times but later was entrusted with the keys to his church, I mustered the courage to stay away."

"You are no coward, Lawrence. Browning is a daunting figure, and he does wield considerable power. I am glad that you are leaving the soldiering to me, while I leave the railroad to you. Yet even I know building that spur to his plantation defies protocol. He must have bribed and or intimidated someone high up."

"He made a not-so-veiled threat as to the consequences of not attending his ceremony. In the case of a madman like Browning, I'd better take his threats seriously."

"He can't be too mad." Corporal Stanton adjusted his pith helmet. "After all, he runs the wealthiest and most productive tea plantation in Assam, and he has the ear of high officials and even royalty."

"That gives his threats gravity. I have new faith in Jesus. Nonetheless, evil has free will."

"Free will but not free reign. For all I know, he may have high-ranking British officers under his thumb." Douglas smiled and looked at Lawrence. "But he doesn't own the entire British Army, and he never will."

"He talks of destroying the world and then renewing it. Even before meeting Mara and receiving Jesus as my Lord and Savior, I was familiar with Armageddon and the New Jerusalem. God determines the hour, not Browning. Yet a man with delusions and the means to put them in motion can wreak considerable havoc and take many innocent lives before he is stopped."

"As for you right now, Lawrence, try not to fret over Browning. The British Army's got your back. We'll see to it he's stopped before his mad schemes go too far. So, cheer up, mate. Think of who you are about to see. Me? I'm thinking about a certain smiling nurse."

"Good point. Love conquers fear. And seeing you want to see Amanda as much as I want to see Mara. What do you say we race? Yahh!" Lawrence yelled as he smacked his horse with his riding crop and galloped away.

"Gee Up!" Douglas shouted at his horse. He quickly gained on Lawrence.

***

Lawrence and Douglas rode through the dusty streets of Sundarpur. The village was quieter and less busy than usual. They passed a few noisy children chasing each other and some stray, clucking chickens. They spotted Amanda on the veranda of the Dak Bungalow. She wore a cream-colored muslin dress. Her wide-brimmed hat shaded the sun from her large, round-framed eyeglasses. She smiled broadly and waved to them. Douglas trotted ahead to greet her. "Amanda! That smile! Its brightness gives the rising sun a run for its money."

"Well, it's a good thing that you saw me before seeing Miss Mara. Her looks cast a shadow on me."

"Nonsense, besides, it's Lawrence who can't take his eyes off of her."

"From what the locals tell me, she's quite soft on the ears too."

"Let Lawrence catch up. We'll all go together and get a good seat in the chapel. Her singing is well worth our early arrival. Blimey! I hope she sings the same Hymn she sang last time I went to her chapel. Lawrence tells me she sang it before hundreds at St. Joseph's Cathedral in Gauhati."

"The St. Joseph's Cathedral? It's huge!" Amanda beamed and spread her palms. "If they invited our Miss Mara to sing there, she must be good."

Lawrence tied his horse next to Corporal Stanton's at the hitching rail and joined them.

"Blimey! Your gal can sing the birds out of their trees." Douglas slapped Lawrence's arm. "Cain't she, mate?"

Lawrence laughed. "Good morning, Amanda. You look chipper this morning."

"Well, this is the day the Lord had made, so let's rejoice and be glad in it." Amanda beamed. "Besides, it's you who's about to see the apple of your eyes and your heart's desire."

Lawrence blushed. "Is it that obvious?"

"Only to someone with an eye." Amanda chuckled. "And God gave me two." Amanda tapped her eyeglasses. "And they work just fine with these."

"We aren't just going to hear Mara sing. Her father is an amazing preacher. Come on." Douglas Stanton motioned toward the Sutcliffe's chapel. "If we keep talking here, we won't get a seat."

Amanda took Douglas's arm and held a parasol over them as they walked toward the chapel. Lawrence followed.

"My brethren," Brian Sutcliffe stood in front of the lectern. "We live in a time when the proud boast of their might, and just as Lucifer in his pride sought to lift his throne above the Almighty's, so too do some men fashion themselves as higher beings. But just as God cast Lucifer from Heaven, so too will pride and delusion bring down the mightiest of men, and God will do so swiftly as an idol of clay shattered beneath an iron rod." Reverend Sutcliffe shook his Bible in his right hand.

"Our Lord and Savior tells us to fear not one who can kill our bodies, but rather fear the one who can destroy both our bodies and souls in Hell. For God tells us in Solomon's proverbs, 'The fear of the Lord is the beginning of wisdom, and knowledge of the Holy is understanding'." He opened his Bible. "Apostle Paul plainly wrote, 'If God be for us, who can be against us?' Our strength is not in a man's sword but the sword of the Spirit. Above all, take the shield of faith, the breastplate of righteousness, and the helmet of salvation. For the blood of Christ makes us righteous, and salvation is his gift. The righteous need not tremble before the proud, for their triumph is brief. The power of the mightiest man is as brief as a shadow that fades with the dawn. But the child of God walks in eternal light."

Reverend Sutcliffe stepped forward and stood between the first two rows of pews. "So let our hearts not be troubled. The Lord, who is for us, will stand beside us in every trial. Have courage, brethren, for while evil roars like a tiger, its time is short." He smiled at the congregation. "For indeed, if God is for us, who can triumph against us?" Reverend Sutcliffe put his Bible on the lectern. "I could deceive you, and you would believe me too, if I told you an angel was about to sing for you." He paused for effect. "But it's only my daughter, Mara." He laughed; the congregation laughed with him.

Mara strode across the chancel and faced the congregation. Leena played the opening notes on the piano. Mara sang,

"You only live once, on this earthly shore,

Your soul is a treasure, worth so much more.

Though sorrows may stay, and years drift away,

One Savior has come to show you the way."

"One life, then eternity,

The cross has won our victory.

Rejoice, he has paid the price,

No second death, but eternal life."

"He calls the lost, through the darkest night,

His mercy is strong; his love shines bright.

The gate is narrow, but the shepherd will guide,

His word shows the way; his arms open wide."

"One life, then eternity,

The cross has won our victory.

Rejoice, he has paid the price,

No second death, but eternal life."

"When shadows falter and dawn appears,

He'll banish all pain and dry all our tears.

A crown of life he will give to all who believe,

and life without end, his children receive."

"One life, then eternity,

The cross has won our victory.

All praise to the risen Son,

The Lamb, our only One."

The congregation was breathless and silent. Reverend Sutcliffe stood next to her and spoke, "You're allowed to cheer. After all, she is my daughter." The congregation gave her a rousing, standing ovation.

After the service, Reverend Sutcliffe stood by the chapel door, shaking hands and offering blessings as his congregation departed. Amanda approached him. Her mouth was circular with the edges raised. "Reverend Sutcliffe," her excitement was palpable. "I am new to the faith. Your message deepened my understanding and stirred something within me. But your daughter," Amanda clasped her hands over her chest. "It was as if Heaven itself descended into your chapel when she sang."

"Thank you, Nurse Fairleigh. I know who you are because Mara told me all about you. God has gifted you as well, just differently."

"Yes, indeed." Amanda beamed. "When I first arrived, I was only a nurse. Now I am more than just a nurse. I am doing the Lord's work, and my reward is far greater than gold. His reward is to the heart and not my purse. You helped me understand that we will always have opposition, but, as the scripture you quoted says, If the Lord is with us, who can triumph against us?"

Corporal Stanton next shook Reverend Sutcliffe's hand. "Thank you for the message, Reverend Sutcliffe. I used to attend services back in Bermondsey, but I've never experienced anything quite like today."

"You're welcome, Corporal. I hope to see you every Sunday." Reverend Sutcliffe turned to Lawrence. "I expected you." He shook Lawrence's hand, placing his left hand over his right hand. "Mara has gone to the dispensary. She wants to be ready in case the heat overwhelms one of our friends and her services are needed." Brian winked at Amanda, "If the worst happens, I'm sure you can lend a hand." He spoke to them while shaking the hand of another attendee. "My wife, Lenna, you all saw her playing the piano, wants you three to join us for lunch. She's preparing her specialty. Curried lamb."

"I'm sure I can answer for all three of us by saying, we'd be honored." Lawrence walked toward the dispensary. Corporal Stanton followed. Amanda grabbed his arm, shook her head, and wagged her finger an inch from her bunched lips. He grinned in response.

Was the other day the beginning of true love, or was it just a moment of passion? Lawrence entered the dispensary with some trepidation. Mara's smile disarmed him. She had slung her wavy black tresses over her left shoulder. Her grandmother's silver cross glistened in the sun.

"Lawrence, I had you meet me here in the clinic." She strode over to him and placed her arms behind his neck. "It wouldn't be proper to kiss you in the chapel, and I don't think the people are ready for us." Mara kissed him on the lips, mingling her tongue with his, relishing the taste of his breath. She breathed through her nose to imbibe every molecule of him. *'I know I should stop, but I can't, and I don't want to.'* She continued to kiss him.

Lawrence held her close. Beyond the loveliness of feeling her body pressed against his and tasting the delicacy of her mouth, an internal surge of passion, delight, and peace filled his being.

At last, their lips separated. "Lawrence, lust is deceitful, but love is understanding. I love you, Lawrence. I never felt this way before, but I know it's my destiny." She kissed him again.

"Mara, it's not of the mind but of the heart. Wise men say that fools rush in where angels fear to tread." He kept his hands on the small of her back. "But wise men never fall in love. I choose to be a fool, a fool in love with you. For only a fool could not love you. Your love gives me a wisdom no book on Earth could teach."

"Close the book on your mind and open your heart." Mara arched her eyebrows. Lovelight beamed. "Kiss me again, Lawrence, and may the love in your heart flow into my heart." Lawrence and Mara tightened their embrace and kissed. Mara pulled back after ten seconds, although she wanted it to last for ten hours. "Lawrence, a thin line exists between love and sin. I know loving you is no sin. My feelings for you are a new and wonderful experience. Acting on my heart and not my mind has blurred my understanding of God's limits. Please, I think we'd better join Amanda and Douglas for lunch with my parents."

"Of course, I would dishonor you if I didn't respect God's boundaries."

Mara took Lawrence's hand and led him from the dispensary. She let go of it after they exited.

***

The noonday sun slanted through the high shutters, laying bright stripes across the Sutcliffes' modest dining room. A teakwood table, polished smooth from years of missionary gatherings, stood with simple porcelain plates and a vase of marigolds that Mara had arranged before the service. The aroma of curried lamb, potatoes, and lentils wafted into the dining room. Amanda smiled at Mara before turning to the Reverend. "I dare say, Reverend Sutcliffe…"

"Call me Brian, as long as I can call you Amanda."

"Okay, Brian." Amanda chuckled. "As I dared to say, your daughter was a delight to the ears, and now your wife is delighting my nose."

"Ahh," Lawrence smiled first at Mara before smiling at Amanda. "If you think Leena's cooking smells good, just wait until you taste it. Brian told us that curried mutton is Leena's specialty. But I know she's set a high bar. I've tasted the fish she cooked after Brian caught it himself in the Brahmaputra River."

"Slicing mutton is far easier than gutting, cleaning, and filleting fish." Mara chuckled and placed her hands on the table.

"Oh, those beautiful hands." Amanda held Mara's right hand and laughed. "I can't imagine them covered in fish guts."

"It's a good thing that I washed my hands." Mara gently squeezed Amanda's hand in return and laughed with her. "I doubt you would be laughing if I rubbed fish guts on your hand."

"Uhh." Amanda playfully shook her hand. She again took Mara's hand and kissed her fingers. "Well, your hand sure doesn't smell or taste like fish guts."

Mara blushed while Brian, Lawrence, and Douglas laughed.

"Blimey! I wager you didn't think British birds had a sense of humor." Douglas took Amanda's hand. "Now you know why England's the poorer and India all the richer for her presence."

"And I wager," Lawrence sniggered, "that you didn't take her hand to check for fish guts."

"Well, if you put it that way, I'd better double-check." Douglas kissed Amanda's hand.

This time, Amanda looked at Mara and blushed.

"And while we're on the topic of fish guts and wagering," Brian tilted his head toward Mara. "I bet you all never guessed that Mara is quite an angler herself. Lawrence, when can you break away from your railway duties?"

"We're going to backtrack and work on a spur near Sundarpur on Thursday. Once the workers get settled, I'm sure the Sirdar and Douglas's men can take it from there."

"Excellent," Brian beamed. "How about Mara and I meet you at the work site, and we go and do some fishing in the Brahmaputra?"

"I've done some fishing in the Schuylkill River in Philadelphia, and once I took the train to Atlantic City and did some saltwater fishing from a pier. But the Brahmaputra? And with Mara?" Lawrence took Mara's hand and smiled at her. "How can I say no?"

From the kitchen came the sound of clinking utensils and a puff of spice-laden air. Leena appeared, cradling a bowl of steaming curried lamb. "Before I make a second trip and bring a bowl of rice, I'd better raise the lid on this so you can smell that it's mutton and not fish guts."

Brian, Mara, Lawrence, and Douglas laughed. Amanda placed her hand on her abdomen, bent over, and guffawed. "I think I can learn a thing or two from you about telling a good lark."

During the meal, Lawrence and Mara exchanged furtive glances and shy smiles. Their fingers sometimes found each other beneath the table. Their quiet affection did not escape Lena's notice.

After Mara had cleared the table, Brian excused himself to his office.

"Mrs. Sutcliffe, I can't remember the last time I ate so well." Corporal Stanton rose and gave a light salute. "Thank you kindly."

Leena smiled. "Amanda, why don't you earn your supper by helping Mara in the clinic?"

"Of course." Amanda returned her smile. "It would be a pleasure to help her." She reached for Mara's hand. "After all, I've much to learn from you."

Mara looked at her mother. She tightened her lips and nodded as Amanda pulled her away by the hand.

"Lawrence," Leena's eyes narrowed slightly, although she again smiled. "Why don't you stay behind and lend me a hand? I may need a man's muscle."

Lawrence, remaining seated, smiled and waved to Mara as she left with Amanda.

Leena sat next to him at the dining room table. "I can tell that you're a trifle nervous. That's a good thing. Your caring about what I think is a sign that your feelings and intentions for my daughter are sincere and honorable. Lawrence, she is my only daughter. While I know that she's no longer a child, I think you understand how I feel. You are the first man to touch her heart. Jesus lives in her heart, of course. Yet her love for God is different. We didn't raise her to be a nun or a celibate. Nuns do wonderful works for God and man. So, maybe it's me who's selfish. We hope for her to one day be a mother and give Brian and me grandchildren. I do not doubt you as a man. You are smart, a hard worker, and a true gentleman. But I do need to ask you an important question."

"Yes, ma'am."

"How do you like India?" She pursed her lips. "Answer honestly. As you know, I am married to an American. I know that you and the British take great pride in your countries. Don't worry about offending me. Be honest."

"Well, for starters, I hate the weather, although I prefer this dry season, or Shika Ritu, over the monsoon, or Boroxa Ritu, season.

"Yes. My husband often talks about America having four seasons. What else do you think of Assam, India?"

"I now have the hang of things, such as the terrain, the natural beauty, the wildlife, and some of your local customs." Lawrence chuckled. "Although I prefer the snakes back home." He laughed. "Our snakes warn you with a rattle before striking."

Leena laughed with him. "Ultimately, you want to go home." Her smile vanished. "Correct?"

"Yes."

"Do you see my concern? If you return to America and abandon Mara, you may wound her heart beyond healing. Should she go through life hurt and bitter, she will never be the same loving, compassionate servant of God." Leena touched Lawrence's hand. "Honor her, Lawrence. Honor her as you would honor God himself. I would rather die a thousand deaths than see you dishonor and abandon my daughter."

Lawrence squeezed her hand and nodded, his eyes saying what a thousand words could never say.

Chapter 17

Lawrence gazed upon the setting sun. A tourmaline haze settled over the horizon, framing another vision of Mara. He signaled to the Sirdar. He blew into his Pepa horn, dismissing the workers. Some workers departed with their tools. Other workers secured the elephants and oxen and stayed in tents on site. Lawrence rode his horse on a side path towards his engineer's quarters near the newly constructed bridge. He heard rifle report.

A dull thud followed, sounding like a heavy bag of rice plopped into the thicket. Lawrence blanched, breath hitching. It was no rice sack. The brush swallowed the man's legs; a black cotton dhoti showed above the leaves. A loop of binding wire was secured under his red kamarband. His dead fingers stiffened on a Katar dagger. Crimson blood flowed from a gunshot wound to the chest. The man lay motionless, his jaw open and still, his dark eyes lifeless and blank. Corporal Stanton galloped up the path, his rifle drawn. He rode over to the fallen man. "Are you all right there, sir?"

"As all right as can be expected after watching a man die in front of me." Lawrence swallowed bile. "I'm not a soldier, so it's not something I'll ever get used to seeing." He removed his hat and wiped sweat from his brow.

"It's not something even hardened soldiers get used to. If they say they do, they're lying, or worse, have lost a piece of themselves. I swore an oath to the king. It's not a matter of letting my conscience decide, I'm afraid. You're in a dangerous place, Lawrence. The king wouldn't have sent me here if it weren't."

Lawrence gazed at the fresh corpse. "Let me get my bearings before I can find a way to thank you for saving my life. His dagger and binding wire were meant for me."

"In the meantime, you'd better start carrying a sidearm. People have been disappearing, and you almost joined them." Corporal

Stanton tensed his lips and sharpened his gaze. "We have your back, but we can't watch you twenty-four hours a day. You are a good man, Lawrence. If it comes down to you or a murderer, make the right choice." He pointed at Lawrence. "You."

Lawrence took a last glance at the fallen assassin.

"I cain't tell you exactly why he tried to assassinate or kidnap you. My guess is politics or religion. You do know that some in India resent British rule and regard your railway as a sacrilege." Corporal Stanton returned his rifle to its sling. "I'd better accompany you to your quarters."

"What about him?" Lawrence pointed to the dead body without looking at it.

"There's nothing for us to do about him. As soon as we arrive at your quarters, I will send a wire to my superiors and report the incident. They'll take care of it. That wasn't the first assassination attempt on a foreigner, or on a native deemed a collaborator, and it won't be the last. In the meantime, let's try to clear our heads and talk of happier things." Douglas smiled. "How about we talk about my smiling nurse or yours with the voice of an angel?"

Lawrence managed a tight smile. "You're right. Better we discuss those who love us rather than those who hate us."

***

A man in a black dhoti with a red kamarband around his waist stood before Sir Nigel. His legs wobbled and his arms prickled; his gut buzzed like a hornet's nest. He had to squeeze his urethra closed.

Browning furrowed his brow and glowered. "I presume you failed to bring me the American."

"Yes…but…Devotee Nagen Barua was shot."

"I hope he is no longer alive."

"I don't know. I think he's dead."

"You think he's dead?" Browning hunched his shoulders. "Living prisoners tend to talk. As a result of your cowardice and failure, we don't have the American; the authorities may have a living, talking suspect; and at the very least, you left behind a uniformed corpse that gives them a clue."

"But the British soldier would have killed me, too, sir. That would give'em two dead bodies."

"Were you not told in the name of the Goddess to kill yourself if you face capture? Two dead bodies are preferable to one talking, living body. Death for Kali is an honor. Instead, you deserted her." Sir Nigel grinned; his eyes like sharpened blades. "Yet the Shiva inside of me has decided to grant you mercy."

The man took a deep breath, sighed, and smiled. "I thank you, all mighty, holy Shiva."

"Yes. You will still attain immortality." Browning paused for effect. "Instead of burning you to ashes, you will serve Kali as a blood sacrifice." Browning sniggered. "Brahman. Take him away."

"No! No! Sir! Please! Please!"

Brahman wrenched the man's arm behind his back and cinched him in a stranglehold. He hauled the man down the corridor. The captive shouted and pleaded, his cries falling on the deaf ears of a laughing Sir Nigel.

Chapter 18

Lawrence, sitting on his horse, double-checked his map. *The terrain is level and obstruction-free for the next mile.* He returned his map to his leather satchel and observed the workers clearing the spur. Their axes and machetes, along with the elephants and oxen, worked in synch. *They're working like a well-oiled machine. I won't be needed for the next mile.*

An ox-led bullock stopped at the fringe of the work site. A man and a woman disembarked. He recognized the light in her eyes a second before the curve of her smile. Mara had a split-cane rod with a brass reel slung over her shoulder. Brian Sutcliffe stood next to her. He shouldered two rods and reels and held a tin tackle box in his right hand. Lawrence totted over to them on his horse. He dismounted and hugged Mara before shaking hands with Brian. "Welcome to the Bengal-Assam railway work site. I'll take those." He took Mara's rod and reel and Brian's tackle box. "My sirdar will set you up with machetes. Go to it."

Mara and Brian laughed.

"I should find you a shovel and have you walk behind the oxen." Brian grinned. "I'll admit you had me going for a couple of seconds," He raised his hands. "After all, I'm sure you'd put me to work, but not my daughter." He turned to Mara and smiled.

"Our Favorite fishing spot on the Brahmaputra is only a short walk away. It's teeming with fish, and," Mara ginned and winked, "none of the crocodiles there want to eat us."

"Hungry or not, crocodiles make me nervous."

"The good news," Brian held up his rod and reel, "is that the fish are hungry. Let's hurry up before the crocodiles eat them all."

***

Here's the best spot. If you can cast your line just below that low branch," Brian pointed, "you will surely catch a rohu and, combining skill, luck, and maybe even divine providence, possibly a catla."

"And this will prove irresistible to any fish." Mara opened their tin bait box. Lawrence blanched at the thick, writhing worms. Mara laughed. "I hope you don't think those worms will swim to the fish by themselves." She pinched a worm between her thumb and forefinger and threaded it onto Lawrence's hook in one smooth motion. "I thought of telling you that the worms bite and have venom stronger than a cobra. I wanted to make you faint so that I would have to give you mouth-to-mouth resuscitation."

"Is it too late to pretend fainting?"

"It's too late to fake passing out, but it's never too late to kiss you." Mara kissed Lawrence's lips.

"Hey, hey, hey." Brian chuckled. "You catch fish with worms, not sugar. I'll never convince you that any fish tastes better. Nevertheless, I came to catch fish. You told me that you fished on the Schuylkill River. Casting a line in the Brahmaputra is no different." Mara got his gear ready. "Let's see if he can put his line under that low branch."

Rod in hand, Lawrence braced his thumb on the reel, flicked his wrist, and put his line directly beneath the low branch.

"Good one, Lawrence." Mara applauded.

"I see you have some practice with this."

"Well, when fishing on the banks of the Schuylkill River, the rowers never offered to take out my line."

"I always enjoyed watching the crew races on the Charles River. Your alma mater, Pennsylvania, always gave Harvard stiff competition. With your build, I'm surprised that you never went out for the crew?"

"I enjoyed fishing on the river, not pulling an oar on it like a galley slave. At Penn, the crew was just as much a social set for the likes of a Cabot as it was a sport. Engineering students without an established last name or their mother's first name on a yacht were seldom invited aboard."

"I thank the Lord that you're just my Lawrence Mills." Mara placed her hand on Lawrence's shoulder and leaned toward him. "If you had a fancy name like Cabot, you might be rowing on the Schuylkill instead of fishing on the Brahmaputra with me."

"And speaking of fishing," Lawrence's rod bent and shook, "I think I got one." He smiled and cranked his reel.

"I see him!" Brian walked over to him. "It's a rohu and a big one!"

Lawrence pulled the fish to shore. Mara placed her rod and reel onto the shore and waded into ankle-deep water. She grabbed the fish, unhooked it, and threaded the fish through the gills onto a chain stringer.

"Mara!" Brian pointed at her rod and reel. "Your rod is trembling! You'd better tend it before a fish pulls your gear into the deep."

Mara grabbed her rod and reel with both hands. The rod bent at a deep arc; the fish strained it into a near half circle. She grimaced and pulled. The instant the rod straightened, she cranked the reel vigorously.

"Did you see that splash?" Brian pointed. "You got a big one!"

Lawrence stepped behind Mara, wrapped his arms around her, and grabbed her rod.

'No. No." Mara gently elbowed him. "This one is all mine." She walked along the bank in the direction of the taut line, cranking her reel faster than her steps. The fish breached the surface.

"It's a catla!" Brian shouted. "A catla! Bring 'em in, Mara! You can do it!"

Mara cranked the reel harder as the fish leapt. The line again tightened. She pulled the rod back with all her strength, gaining two seconds to crank the reel and bring the fish closer. The catla still fought. Mara's muscles burned, her joints stiffened, and she gasped for breath. Mara spotted both Lawrence and her father approaching her. She shook her head and lipped, "No," without speaking. Grimacing, she pulled and cranked even harder. The catla was now feet away from her. Mara waded into the river, grabbed the line, and lifted the fish. She beamed at Lawrence and her father.

"You did it, Mara!" Brian applauded. "You did it! You caught a catla and a big one."

Mara handed Lawrence the line. She sat on the riverbank with her legs crossed, gasping for breath. He held the fish aloft. "Even I can barely lift this thing. Every moment you surprise me more, and every moment I love you more."

Brian half-smiled.

"A catla is a rare fish." Mara beamed. "We've caught more rohu than I care to clean and enough to feed an army. He fought a brave fight. I say we spare him. Lawrence, please pull the hook and let him go."

"I agree. He's a beaut'. He'll look far better in the river than on a platter." Lawrence extracted the hook, placed the fish in the water, and smiled as the catla swam away.

"Well, we've caught more than we need, and we have a long walk home. So, what do we say we call it a day?"

"I agree." Mara took Lawrence's hand. "If we call it a day, it gives me enough time to take you to my favorite place." She turned to Brian. "Is it okay with you, father?"

"Go on without me. I'll take care of our tackle and catch. I still have time to catch a ride on a bullock cart."

∗∗∗

Lawrence and Mara sat together on a hilltop. "This was my favorite place as a child. It was always a treat when my parents took me here. As a little girl, I could never go alone, and for good reasons. Now that I have you for company, it's even more special."

"I can understand why you cherish this place." Lawrence lay back. "We can see everything from here. The river…and even the distant mountains. Now that I am with you, I can appreciate the beauty of Assam. Yet nothing can top the beauty of the one whose hand I'm holding. I love you, Mara."

"I love you too, Lawrence." Mara lay her head on Lawrence's chest, tapped his nose, and kissed his cheek. "You may not have realized a special moment, and it had nothing to do with catching a catla. You said that beautiful word to me in front of my father."

"Beautiful word?" Lawrence held Mara even tighter.

"Love, silly. You told me that you loved me in front of my father." Mara pulled his hand to her mouth and nibbled on his fingers. "My parents are wise. They know that I love you and you love me. Maybe earlier, if you had said it in front of my father, it might have made me feel uneasy. Yet today your words were music to my ears. And best of all," she kissed Lawrence's cheek, "my father seemed to enjoy it too." She smiled. "But not a fraction as much as I enjoyed it." She lifted her head to him and pressed her mouth to his in a long, unhurried, tender kiss.

"Oh, Mara, I have loved before, but until I met you, I never knew nor tasted true love."

"Only you and I together will learn the true melody of love."

138

Lawrence and Mara held each other tight, their two hearts a breath apart, their mouths joined in a loving kiss. Tenderness swelled into passion; they clung to one another, blind to everything until the ground slipped beneath them. Locked together, they rolled down the hill. At the bottom, they lay tangled; their breathless laughter spiced and sweetened their kisses. Mara didn't notice that her blouse buttons had come undone. His lips lowered. She combed her fingers through the hair at his nape, hearing her own soft cries as if from outside herself. "No! No!" She pushed his head away. "Stop." She stood and turned away. She hastily buttoned up her blouse. "We let our feelings go too far." Mara turned and prodded. "You'd better go."

"But it's not safe to leave you alone."

"I'll be fine, Lawrence. There's still plenty of daylight. The main road is nearby. It's safe enough." She drew a shaky breath. We need time apart to pray. What happened was wrong." Mara turned and walked towards the main road.

"Mara, I'm sorry. I love you."

Mara did not look back.

***

Mara stood by her front door. *Lord Jesus, I know I've asked a thousand times, but I ask again. Please forgive me for what happened with Lawrence. I love him, but I know we're still unmarried and we have sinned.* An oppression like a thick fog enveloped Mara as she entered her home. Her mother sat on a living room chair. Mara avoided making eye contact.

"You're back. Isn't your father with you?"

Mara bowed her head. "No, mother. He left before us."

"Well," Leena stood. "If he left before you, he should be here. I worried a bit about you, but I knew you were with your father and Lawrence. Your father should be here." She lowered her

139

head. "I know this is wrong, and I should trust in the Lord, but I have a bad feeling. He was alone, and bad things have been happening in our area."

"Please don't worry, mother." Mara raised her head but did not make eye contact with Leena. "Father has often traveled alone. I'm sure he's fine."

"Yes. I know." Leena tensed her lips. "But he's seldom late."

Mara wrestled the hillside from her mind; her last look at her father took its place. She pinched her eyes shut. *Did my sinning put my father in danger?*

"Please pray with me, Mara."

Mara and Leena faced each other, holding hands. Mara buried her face into her mother's shoulder; her tears soaked her blouse.

"Heavenly father," Leena prayed. "Please let the Holy Spirit shield Brian from all danger, whether from man or beast. Amen."

"Amen." Mara ran to her bedroom, collapsed face down on her bed, and cried into her pillow. *If you must, punish me, Lord, I accept your judgment. But please don't punish my father for my sin.* Mara cried until she fell asleep.

Mara awoke in the middle of the night. After climbing out of bed, she walked to her living room. Her mother was awake, sitting on a chair. Sweat beads and teardrops covered her face. She pressed her hands together tight as a vice. Her jaw chattered in silent prayer. Mara knelt beside her and kissed her cheek. They cried together.

Chapter 19

The nape of Brian's neck tingled as if it were from marching ants. He rubbed his neck with a handkerchief, only wiping away sweat. His ears pricked like a hound catching a scent. He looked around. No twigs breaking or leaves rustling. *Something's not right. Be with me, Lord. Be with me.*

Reverend Sutcliff never saw them. Two men wearing black dhotis with red kamarbands around their waists pounced from behind with a leopard's stealth. One wrenched Brian's arm behind his back, cinched him in a stranglehold, and shoved him face-first to the ground. The other thug gagged him with a cloth, secured his wrists, and then his ankles with binding wire, winding it tight enough to cut through the outer layers of his skin. Afterward, he jammed his knee into the small of Brian's back. The other thug left to retrieve a donkey tied to a tree hidden in the jungle. Every movement, even the slightest twitch, shot tendrils of pain through Brian's wrists, ankles, and nerves. The thug returned with a donkey carrying a canvas tarp. The two shrouded Brian in the tarp, wrapped four ropes around him, and tied the covering down tightly. They next hoisted Brian onto the donkey and led the donkey for a half mile down the path until reaching a dual horse-drawn wagon waiting on the main road. After the thugs tossed Brian into the wagon, the driver cracked his whip.

The two horses pulled the wagon down the road with a synchronized trot. Brian prayed, *Heavenly Father, in the name of Jesus, may the Holy Spirit protect Leena and Mara.*

***

Reverend Sutcliff sat on the floor in a windowless, whitewashed room's corner. The only light came from a hallway torch, its glow creeping through the bars of the door. The binding wires were gone from his wrists and ankles, but dark red grooves remained as a painful reminder of his ordeal.

Brahman inserted a skeleton key into the door lock, turned, and opened the door. Nigel Browning entered the cell. "If this were a zoo, the placard on your cage would read a single word: Fool."

Brian remained seated, feeling dwarfed as Browning loomed over him. "Who's the fool? You were foolish enough to sell your soul to Satan without even realizing it. Only a fool would believe he is more than a man. You're deluded and the worst of fools." Brian pointed. "What's more foolish than mistaking madness for wisdom?"

Browning lurched over to him. "Who is the mad and deluded one? Believing that a dead Jewish carpenter from 1,900 years ago can give you immortality?" He smirked. "Now you sit like the lowest of condemned prisoners." He put his hands on his hips and looked down at Brian. "Use your final hours to contemplate what you could've had. I offered more wealth than you ever imagined. As the mortal father of Kali's earthly form, you would've been honored among men and Gods."

"My daughter is not some commodity for sale, and as a precious child of the one true God, she would never partake in your madness."

"Ha! Ha! Ha!" Browning laughed from the depths of Hell. "Ha! Ha! Ha! Your daughter will soon intimately know the Goddess who dwells within her. She will rise as Kali incarnate. As Kali, she will marry me and empower Shiva inside me. Together, we will destroy, redeem, and rule forever."

"The only immortality you're getting is an eternity in Hell, and you won't rule so much as the ashes of the damned."

'Silence!" Browning cocked his foot to kick him. "I should punish your insolence this instant." He relaxed his foot, straightened, and let out a low, ugly laugh. "Ha! Ha! Ha! I am a patient man- a gentleman of restraint. I can wait, for your hour draweth nigh." He tilted his head and sneered. "How ironic. Your seed created the Goddess's earthly form. This evening, your blood will rouse her Heavenly form from slumber." Browning raised his chin. "Until then, pray to your Jewish carpenter. See if he saves you; see if he stops the inevitable. Once Kali is awakened, all worshipers of lesser Gods will bend their knee to her."

Browning exited the cell. He nodded to Brahman to lock the door and muttered, "Keep an eye on this blasphemer. It will be a pleasure to give him what he has coming."

Brian steepled his hands and prayed. "Thank you for dying for my many sins and saving my soul. I surrender my fate to you. I beg you to spare Leena and Mara from Browning's Satanic scheme. Amen."

Chapter 20

Lawrence sat on horseback observing workers dump fill from a four-oxen-led cart. Chittagong was no longer a distant dream but an approaching reality. "Blimey! Do you look lost in thought?" Corporal Stanton rode over to Lawrence. "I cain't say I blame ya."

"Mara is surely a more pleasant thought than the railway." Lawrence half-smiled. "Nevertheless, duty calls. I must focus on the task at hand."

"I hear what you're saying. It's hard for me to keep my mind off a certain smiling nurse."

"The difference is that the railway gets built even if I do lose myself in thought. But I would be dead right now if, last week, you resided in dreamland."

"Amanda is more than a daydream, Lawrence. I knew from the first day we met at the Deptford and Bermondsey library that she was the lass for me. It's about timing. I'm gonna ask her. But first I need to figure out when she'll say yes."

"Are you sure about loving her at first sight?" Lawrence chuckled. "Before I even saw Mara, you painted a portrait of her with words so vivid that it would make Dante green with envy." Lawrence lowered his head and grimaced at the memory of Mara turning her back on him.

"You got me there, mate." Corporal Stanton smiled. "But Dante was Italian. My countryman John Keats wrote almost ninety years ago: *A thing of beauty is a joy forever.* And isn't poetry a good way to win a young lady's heart? Didn't I say that Amanda was not as ravishing as Mara? Yet Amanda is plenty bonny, and she's just right for me."

"I can second that. Amanda surely charmed Mara and her parents. Me too, if you must know, and I know you're right for her. I'll say a little prayer for you two." Lawrence half-smiled. "Until then, we'd better get back to work."

***

The seemingly endless day ended. Lawrence signaled to the Sirdar to dismiss the workers. Lawrence rode to the nearby Dak Bungalow, secured his horse, and went to his room. He collapsed onto his knees, folded his hands, and knelt over his bed. "Oh Lord, forgive me, not only have I sinned against you, but I dishonored Mara and caused her to sin. Oh Lord, I love her. I love her so much." Lawrence opened his eyes and looked upward. He closed his eyes. "Yes, Lord, I want to marry her. If you would show me grace and make it possible, I will propose to her the next time I see her."

145

Chapter 21

Time had ceased to exist for Brian Sutcliffe. The deep grooves from the binding wire had swollen and turned from red to a grotesque shade of purple and black. Pain burned in the bones beneath his buttocks after hours sitting on the stone floor, while his lower spine had stiffened and ached from the strain. Sweat and tears had dried on his face as he had prayed nonstop for his wife and daughter. Any semblance of rest escaped him. He jerked his head up on hearing keys jingling. Four men wearing black dhotis with red kamarbands entered his cell, lifted him, and forced him down the hallway. Brian knew that it was his last walk. He said aloud, "The Lord is my shepherd, I shall not want. He maketh me lie down in green pastures, he leadeth me beside still waters. He leadeth me in the paths of righteousness for his name's sake. Yea, though I walk through the valley of the shadow of death, I will fear no evil: for thou art with me."

Browning's thugs forced him to stand on a wooden platform flanked by ropes and pulleys. Two chains ending in manacles hung from an overhead beam. A thug seized each of his swollen wrists, wrenched his arms upward, and clicked the manacles shut.

"Surely your goodness and mercy are still with me, and soon I shall dwell in your house forever."

They tore off his shirt, rubbed it in his face, and threw it aside.

"The Lord is my rock, my fortress, and my deliverer in whom I take refuge. You are my shield and the horn of my salvation and stronghold."

An adjacent platform attached to ropes and pulleys waited ten feet away. Marco Bellini wore acolyte attire consisting of a maroon dhoti, black kamarband, and a maroon sleeveless kurta with a black stole. He stood beside the figurine that he had sculpted for Sir Nigel. He tugged its pure white silk shroud down an inch, beamed, and walked away.

Sir Nigel Browning stood on his Temple's chancel. He wore a pure white silk dhoti with a broad, crimson kamarband holding a gold katar dagger. Gold buttons secured his black silk waistcoat. He raised his arms. "Acolytes, the World's destruction draweth nigh. The eve of my ascension to Shiva is at hand. The Goddess is awakening from her slumber."

The congregation chanted, "Kali, Kali, blessed thee; Kali, Kali, blessed thee; Kali, Kali, blessed thee."

Browning held up his arms to silence the congregation. "You will soon behold the sire of her mortal form. He blasphemed the Goddess and betrayed his daughter. Only his ultimate sacrifice will redeem him and earn her forgiveness. His blood will awaken the Goddess." With his foot, Browning triggered a charge. Smoke boiled upward from the floor, cloaking the chancel. Thugs in the lower level hurriedly pulled on ropes, raising the platforms with Brian Sutcliffe and the shrouded figurine.

Reverend Sutcliff, gagged and wrists manacled to chains hanging from an above beam, faced the congregation.

"Now! Behold! The Goddess!" Browning pulled away the shroud.

The congregation chanted, "Kali, Kali, blessed thee; Kali, Kali, blessed thee; Kali, Kali, blessed thee."

The figurine matched her height, limb lengths, and curves to the exact centimeter. Every line of her face, the set of her eyes and lips, even the fall of her hair, was flawless. The statue enshrined Mara.

"Kali, Kali, blessed thee; Kali, Kali, blessed thee; Kali, Kali, blessed thee."

Brian thrust his head forward and tried to scream through the gag. The red veins in his eyes popped. He vainly fought his chains.

Browning lifted a gold chalice from the lectern and held it up to the congregation before drawing the gold katar from his kamarband. He turned to Brian, narrowed his eyes, grinned, and laughed. Holding the dagger before him, Sir Nigel tilted the blade to catch the light of oil lamps hanging from the ceiling and flashed it into Brian's eyes. With a backhand sweep, Browning slashed his throat; blood filled his chalice. "The Goddess shall live!" Sir Nigel shouted as he hurled the blood over the Mara statue.

"Kali, Kali, blessed thee. Kali, Kali, blessed thee. Kali, Kali, blessed thee."

Sir Nigel raised his arms to silence the congregation. "Prince Alaric of Schwatzenheim," Browning pointed. "Kali wants to adopt you as her son, Skanda."

The congregation again chanted, "Kali, Kali, blessed thee; Kali, Kali blessed thee; Kali, Kali, blessed thee."

The prince stepped up to the chancel. Browning handed him the katar and chalice. Prince Alaric grabbed Brian's inert head by the hair, lifted it, and looked at Browning.

Browning nodded.

With a smile, the Prince of Schwatzenheim slashed a second cut to his throat, filled the chalice with his blood, and heaved it over the figurine.

The congregation chanted fervently. "Kali, Kali, blessed thee. Kali, Kali, blessed thee. Kali, Kali, blessed thee."

"Fredrick Robert Upcott, Chairman of Kali's iron road." Browning's commanding voice rose above the crowd. "Come forth and claim your godhood as Kubera. The iron road shall serve as the veins of Kali's destruction and renewal.

The railway chairman took the katar and chalice from the prince. Upcott clenched his teeth, tightened his lips, and smiled. With wide eyes, he repeatedly drew back the dagger before thrusting it downward, ripping open his chest and abdomen. Violent urges sated, Upcott collected Brian's blood into the chalice and splashed it over the idol.

Browning announced. "Behold, I rise as Shiva." He strolled to the Mara idol and planted a prolonged kiss on its lips. Smoke again cloaked the chancel as the platform sank, lowering Browning and the idol out of sight.

The congregation's chant reached fever pitch, "Shiva, Shiva, death and night and blood. Shiva, Shiva, death and night and blood. Shiva, Shiva, death and night and blood."

****

Under the cover of clouds on a moonless night, two thugs lugged Brian Suttcliffe's wrapped body down to the riverbank. At Browning's order, they had tied stones to his ankles and waist. Twenty yards upstream, they propped his fishing rod in the mud and set his tackle box beside it.

"Crocodiles will finish the rest." One of the thugs muttered as he tossed his torn, blood-soaked shirt into the river. The thugs next heaved the body into the black water. It slipped under without a splash, swallowed by the current.

Chapter 22

The sweat and tears had long since dried from Mara's face. Leena sat in near catatonia. "Please, Mother, we'll keep praying until Father comes home." Mara kept her arm wrapped around her. "Have faith. He will come home. Until then, please, at least drink some broth. You haven't eaten or drunk anything in three days." Mara kissed her cheek. "Let's take comfort in our Lord's promise, Mother. All things work together for the good of those who love the Lord."

Three hard knocks rattled the door.

"Remain here." Mara squeezed her mother and touched her cheek to hers. "I'll get it." Mara opened the door. She gasped. Her heart dropped into the pit of her gut. Blood drained from her face; her expression looked like a waxwork's.

On the threshold stood a tall, fair-skinned priest in a long black cassock, a silver cross resting on his chest. Behind him stood two Assamese magistrates in pressed khaki uniforms and polished boots. One of the magistrates held Brian's fishing gear.

Tears spilled down Mara's cheeks.

"I am sorry, my child." The priest dabbed at a tear on his own cheek with a handkerchief. "Your father went to the river to fish. We found his rod and tackle on the bank. There were signs of a struggle. Downstream, they recovered his torn, bloodstained shirt. Fish are abundant in those waters. Unfortunately, so are Crocodiles. My child," he laid his hands on her shoulders. "I'm sorry, but the police concluded that crocodiles took his mortal body." The priest raised his head, fresh tears ran down his cheek, "but Jesus holds his immortal soul."

'No!" Mara covered her face with her hands; tears streamed through her fingers. She turned to her mother. Leena had slid limp in her chair. Her eyes were closed, her breathing faint.

"Mother! Mother!" Mara dropped to her knees in front of Leena and clasped her hands. "Mother!" Her voice broke. "Oh Lord Jesus! I am sorry I had sinned with Lawrence. Why was my father punished for my sins?" She cried out her words in blind grief. "But please spare my mother."

The Priest stepped over and laid his hand on Leena's inert shoulders. "The Mother of our Lord knelt at the foot of the cross as he died a horrible death." He said softly. "She knows your sorrow." Leena still did not stir. The priest bowed his head. "May the Father, the Son, and the Holy Ghost comfort you."

Mara remained on her knees and cried into Leena's lap.

Chapter 23

Lawrence began his journey with the rising sun. He stopped to admire a multicolored chameleon lapping dew from a broad, emerald leaf. "What is the color of love, my four-legged friend. You can change colors on demand, but the heart of this man is set on one woman alone. I love her forever, and unlike your colors, I am powerless to change it." Lawrence nudged his horse with his boot. "Giddyup, Raja!" They galloped down the trail. He pulled back on the reins to pass under the low branch of a champak. The tree dropped soft golden petals on him. He smiled at the petals resting on his shirt, glistening in the morning sun; He raised his nose to imbibe its intoxicating perfume. Thoughts of Mara became so intense that he again experienced every tactile sensation of his final moments with her, as well as the sight and taste of her forbidden loveliness. *Yes. I must marry her.* His horse shifted from hoof to hoof and tossed its head, bit clicking between its teeth, breaking Lawrence's reverie. "Woe, Raja," He pulled back on the reins. A leopard appeared on the trail's fringe. Lawrence's nerves tensed.

I know how dangerous you can be, but what a privilege to see you. I know a sleek lightweight like you has no interest in a two-hundred-pound man and a thousand-pound horse. Lawrence relaxed and rode beside the cat. He admired both the beauty of its fur and form, as well as the perfect coordination of its gait and muscles. His horse neighed and stood on its rear hooves. The leopard bolted into the thicket.

***

By mid-afternoon, Lawrence rode along the dusty main road of Sundarpur. Something wasn't right, but his mind couldn't fathom it. His vision was blurry; the sun seemed to cloud the vista with an orange haze. People who usually noticed him as an American stranger were oddly oblivious. Even the stray chickens and goats were quiet and orderly. *There it is.* He smiled on seeing the Sutcliffes' front door. He dismounted and secured his horse. *What if she's still angry with me? Our final moments were so pleasurable but so wrong. I know I dishonored her. We sinned, but I can make it right. I want to marry her more than anything I've ever wanted.* He stood at the threshold of her home. He closed his eyes and prayed. "Lord Jesus, in the name of the Father, please forgive me for causing Mara to sin, and please move on her heart to forgive me." He tensed his lips and looked upward. "And if it be your will, please move on her heart to accept my proposal."

Lawrence gently rapped on their door. Mara answered. The smile he had hoped for never came. Mara's face looked drained, her eyes swollen and glassy, as if the days apart had drained every tear from her and left nothing but a stunned, hollow calm. Lawrence spotted Leena in his peripheral vision. She sat in a stupor, failing to notice him. Her pallid complexion, dried tears, and gauntness told him that something was wrong, very wrong. "Mara, talk to me." Lawrence grabbed her shoulders. "What's wrong?"

Tears filled Mara's eyes. She dropped her head, looking away from him.

"Mara, please."

She raised her head and met his eyes. "Lawrence. My father is dead."

"No! No! My precious Mara." Lawrence pulled her into his arms and held her.

Mara wrapped her arms around him and sobbed on his shoulder. After five seconds, she pushed him away, walked over to Leena, and held her hand. "Mother, look, Lawrence is here."

Leena turned and looked at Lawrence. She did not smile or speak.

Lawrence walked over to them. "I am mortified. Please…If there is anything I can do…"

Mara massaged Leena's hand. "You've done enough already."

"What do you mean? I love you, Mara, and I loved Brian like a second father."

"You don't know, Lawrence." Mara's voice broke. "You just don't know. After we left my father alone and went to the hill, he returned to the river to catch more fish. While we were lost in lust, crocodiles tore him to pieces. They only found his bloodied and tattered shirt."

"They didn't find his body." Lawrence spread his palms. "Maybe we still have hope."

"No, Lawrence. They also found his fishing gear. It was his prized possession. He would never abandon it. We caught enough fish. If we stayed with him instead of leaving to sin, he never risks going to that stretch of river at dusk."

"We can't blame ourselves for mindless reptiles," Lawrence said softly. "Yes, Mara. We lost ourselves in each other, but we stopped short of, well, you know. Mara, our love will never be sinful again. Marry me. I love you, and I will love you forever. Marry me, and we can name our first son, Brian."

"Marrying you would keep us from future sin, but it will not bring back my father." Mara shook her head. "Lawrence, we are from two different worlds. You are older than I am. You have known love before, and, from how you speak of Dorothy, you've also known the pleasures of the flesh." She blushed and lowered her eyes. "I confess that I have thought about such things since I was much younger. Yet you are the first man that I have ever loved, ever touched, or allowed to touch me. Soon, the railway will reach Chittagong. You will go home to your world. I am confused now. I am even doubting my faith. I think you should go."

Lawrence tensed his lips, nodded, and turned toward the door. "I love you. Mara." He stepped out and closed the door behind him.

Mara fell to her knees before her mother. "I love him, Mother. I love him. Why did I send him away?"

Leena squeezed her daughter's hand in return.

<h1 align="center">Chapter 24</h1>

Mara mustered the best approving smile she could for Leena. "I could never cook as well as you, Mother. But seeing you eat gives me a little joy in our great sorrow."

"Our Lord fasted for forty days and nights, but we need our strength to serve him." Leena nodded without smiling.

"Spiritual as well as physical strength, mother." Mara took Leena's hand. "We are Christians, not pagans. Jesus said, *Blessed are those who mourn, for they shall be comforted.* Yet we must not succumb to ancestor worship or turn Brian into an idol. We are not without hope, mother. Come with me. Let's pray and read God's word on the matter.

Mara and Leena continued to hold hands. They closed their eyes and bowed their heads. "Lord Jesus, we thank the Father in Your name for filling our hearts with the Holy Ghost and for comforting us as we mourn our father and husband. We pray for greater understanding as we gather to read your Word." Mara opened her Bible. "Mother, let me read you from 1 Thessalonians, verses 13 to 18. Mara's final memory of her time with Lawrence before her father's death made her wince while reading verses 3-7 to herself. *For this is the will of God, your sanctification, that you abstain from sexual immorality. That each one of you know how to control his own body in holiness and honor, not in the passion and lust like the Gentiles who do not know God; that no one transgress and wrong his brother in this manner, because the Lord is an avenger in all these things, as we told you beforehand and solemnly warned you. For God has not called us for impurity, but in holiness.* Mara closed her eyes and asked God for forgiveness before she read aloud 1 Thessalonians verses 13 to 18 to her mother.

"But we do not want you to be uninformed, brothers, about those who are asleep, that you may not grieve as those who have no hope. For since we believe that Jesus died and rose again, even

156

so, through Jesus, God will bring with him those who have fallen asleep. For this, we declare to you the word of the Lord that we who are alive, who are left until the coming of the Lord, will not precede those who have fallen asleep, for the Lord himself will descend from Heaven with a cry of command, with the voice of an archangel and with the sound of the trumpet of God. And the dead in Christ will rise first. Then we who are alive, who are left, will be caught up together with them in the clouds to meet the Lord in the air, and we will always be with the Lord. Therefore, encourage one another with these words."

"We will remain strong in the faith. Mara. I know we will be with Brian again. Of course, it will be different. Our vows were until death do us part. In Heaven, we will not marry or be given into marriage. But be like angels of God." A tear glistened in Leena's eyes as she smiled at Mara. "When the time is right, we will all be reunited. Until then, I shall miss him. I miss him with all my heart."

The sixth verse, *God is an avenger in all these things*, tolled in Mara's mind like a funeral bell. She looked away and squeezed her eyes shut, fighting back tears as she thought, *My misunderstanding of him and his ways is like viper venom: burning, destructive, deadly. But did he strike my father because of my sin?*

A gentle rap on the door broke Mara's reverie. A teen boy wearing a white dhoti stood at the door. "A post for you, memsahib." He handed Mara a sealed envelope with a London return address.

"Thank you, young man." Mara took the letter and pressed a baksheeth coin in his palm.

The boy smiled and slightly bowed before departing.

"Mother. It's from the Baptist Foreign Missions Board in London." Mara opened the letter and read it. She lowered her eyes and frowned.

"Mara? Mara?" Leena's jaw chattered. "It's not more bad news, is it?"

"Mother, I'm sorry, yes. It's bad news, but not unexpected." Mara tensed her lips. "I'll read it for you. They send their sincere condolences for our loss while assuring us that Brian has joined the Heavenly angels in eternal life." Mara saw the tightening in Leena's mouth and new creases in her brow. "I'll get to the point." Mara sat across from Leena and held both of her hands. "The Baptist Foreign Missions Board has chosen Brian's replacement. His name is Patrick Kiernan. His wife's name is Kathlene. He's originally from New York City, but he's served in several missionary posts here in India. They will arrive next week." Mara's eyes clouded. "We can stay in the house," her voice broke, "but only as paid servants."

"No, Mara, no." Leena released Mara's hands and raised and shook her own. "That's unacceptable! We've lived here since before you were born. God called me to serve him, not be a house servant."

"It's unfair, Mother. But we knew this would happen. I am willing to meet the Kiernan's household needs. After all, the school children need me, and the community needs me in the dispensary. Oh, mother, you have made me what I am. You have loved me, nurtured me, and educated me. But I am an adult now. I will understand if you choose to leave."

"Mara, my husband was torn from my side. I don't know if I can bear separating from my daughter. But I know I cannot suffer living here and watching another couple soil my memories of Brian, my pregnancy, and my raising you from a baby and your brother Christopher's early years."

"Mother, I wrote to him about what happened." Mara tensed her lips and fought back tears. "He won't even know for another month. I don't even want to think about his agony when reading the letter."

"We can fast and pray over this, Mara, yet my decision will not change. Your brother may offer to return from Boston. We can't let him do that. He has built a new life for himself. I must leave and live with my family in Calcutta."

Mara and Leena rose and met each other's gaze. They embraced and wept together.

Chapter 25

Mara and Leena stood together on the Sundarpur wharves. The launch steamer belched a smoke plume. The first mate sounded the boat's horn in a long, sharp blast. Mara fought back tears and sniffled. "They're about ready to leave, Mother. Please. Stay."

"Mara, my precious, beautiful daughter, I was about to beg you to come and live with me in Calcutta. My darling dear, you are an adult now. The Sundarpur Children and the community depend on you. Our Lord needs you to serve them. You can't forsake the children and the village for a grieving mother." Leena tightened her lips. "You will never know how much you have helped me." Leena placed her hands on Mara's shoulders and smiled. "God knows how much. Now you need to devote yourself to serving him. Leave the rest of my recovery to my family in Calcutta."

Mara and Leena embraced. The ship's horn blasted. Leena pulled away, held both of Mara's hands, and kissed her forehead. "Goodbye, Mara. I promise to write every day, and I will pray for you every moment."

"I love you, Mother."

"I love you too, Mara." Leena turned and walked up the gangplank. She turned and waved one last time after entering the launch steamer and disappearing into the crowd of passengers.

Mara wailed as the boat chugged down the Brahmaputra River.

***

Mara rode home on the edge of the bullock cart, her sobbing spent, her body still slumped and empty. At the gate, she climbed down, walked the remaining yards home, and strode through her front door. She steeled herself against the emptiness that awaited her.

"You don't believe in knocking?" Kathleen Kiernan lurched toward her with a glowering face and prodding finger.

Mara gasped. The woman confronting her stood an inch taller and outweighed her by a good hundred pounds. She was broad-shouldered with wide, fleshy arms wobbling with every movement. Her stout torso made her legs appear shorter. "But this is my house," Mara tilted her head.

"Now, K.K.," Patrick Kiernan rose from his chair. He stood several inches shorter than his wife, with a belly round like a cauldron and arms thin like reeds. A low, bulbous nose, reddened and crinkled, with fine veins sat above jowls hanging like soiled cleaning rags. "She must be Mara Sutcliffe. She still lives here, you know."

"She may still live here," Katheen put her hands on her hips and thrust her jaw toward her husband. "But she needs to know her place."

"My belongings..." Mara cringed upon seeing her possessions stacked against the far wall like freight waiting to be loaded onto a train. "...You even went through my personal effects. You had no right..."

"I had no right? Just where do you think you are, young lady?" Kathleen scowled and prodded at Mara. "You of all people should know better." She put her hands on her hips. "You're in Raj India, not the United States. Here, you have no rights."

"You even took down my father's portrait." Mara pointed to her father's portrait, now just another item stacked with her belongings.

"We made room for our dear departed daughter, Karen." Patrick pointed to the portrait that took Brian's place. The replacement was a framed picture of a cherubic, platinum-haired ten-year-old girl wearing a white dress and holding a daisy under her nose.

"She's your lesson in sacrifice." Kathlene jutted her jaw at Mara. "She can teach you what a real missionary must endure. I lost a child. Dead from malaria while we conducted our duties. Not a middle-aged man getting himself killed because of a fishing outing. I'll let you put your father's portrait up in your servant's room. But keep it there. And another thing. You will only dress in white. This is a missionary house, not a whore house. Now move your things to the servant's room. We eat breakfast at eight am. I expect it to be on time."

Mara glared into Kathleen's pinched eyes and scanned her fleshy face, capped with brittle curly black hair and centered with a pug nose. An image of Varaha, Vishnu's boar-headed idol, flashed into her mind. *Lord Jesus, forgive me for letting a foreign God haunt me.*

Mara walked away. She prayed while gathering her possessions and moving them into the servant's room. She hung the portrait of her father over her bed before folding her personal attire and putting them in a chest of drawers and hanging her clothes in the closet. After making her bed, she collapsed face-first onto it and cried into her pillow. "Lord Jesus, I miss my father and now my mother. Please bless and protect her. Why did I send Lawrence away? I know we sinned, but I miss him too. Oh, Lord, I confess, I love him."

Chapter 26

Mara wore her white dress with her grandmother's silver cross around her neck. She served Kathleen Keirnan a poached egg.

"This is undercooked. I thought I told you that I loathe undercooked eggs." Kathleen dropped her fork on her plate. "Cook it again."

Mara scooped up the poached egg with a spatula and walked it over to the oven. Patrick Keirnan's lips twisted upward; his eyes stalked her every move. Kathleen watched them both like a bird of prey from a perch. Mara returned with the fully cooked egg. As she tried to scoop it onto Kathlene's plate, she scowled and glared at her. Mara's hands jittered; the egg slipped off the spatula and plopped onto the floor.

"You clumsy, worthless oaf." Kathleen stood and jabbed her finger at Mara. "Clean that up, now!"

Mara fetched a whisk broom and dustpan from the kitchen corner. She bent over and swept the splattered egg into the dustpan.

Kathleen spotted her husband watching her with eyes widening, bright as a yolk in the morning light. His grin crept almost to his ears.

"Forget about it!" Kathleen screamed and prodded at Mara. "You've cost me my appetite anyway. Go to your room!" She pointed at the door to the servant's room.

Mara stood, squared her shoulders, and glared at Kathleen. Mara turned and walked out the front door.

Kathleen snatched the frying pan and, with a backfisted swing, bashed the flat end of it against her husband's eye.

Sparks exploded across Patrick's vision; pain boomed through his skull like a hammered gong.   Stunned, he clamped both hands over the wound.

"That's your last look at that disobedient hussy." Kathleen planted the frying pan at her hip like a Wild West gunslinger. "She is on borrowed time here, I'm telling you, and so are you if so much as glance at her again."

Patrick kept his hand over his eye. "I wasn't looking at her, K.K." Pain still radiated in his skull.

"You're a pig! An adulterous swine. I saw you stripping her with those lustful eyes. You're supposed to be a man of God. The word you preach says that just looking at a woman in lust is to commit adultery with her." Kathleen leveled the frying pan at the front door, aiming it like a pistol. "Now go to the chapel and prepare for Sunday. And remember, if your eye causes you to sin, pluck it out. It's better to go to Heaven blind than burn in hell."

Patrick bent back with his hand pressed against the wound.

"Now!" She wielded the frying pan in his face.

Patrick skulked out of the house and crept to his office in the chapel. He opened his desk drawer and placed a glass on the desktop. In the lower drawer, he kept what he wanted. A bottle of Paddy Whiskey. After opening it, he looked at the glass. He changed his mind. He chugged the contents straight from the bottle.

Mara straightened out medicine bottles in a dispensary cabinet. She sang the John Newton hymn, *Amazing Grace,* while she worked.

Patrick spoke to his Whiskey bottle. "I came to you to wash away the Devil. It sounds like you sent me an angel." He stood and staggered to the dispensary. "Thank you."

Mara gasped at the black, blue, and purple welt around Patrick's eye. Tiny beads of pus and blood oozed from swollen flesh. "What happened to you?"

"I slipped and hit my head on the table."

"I'd better clean that up for you." Mara patted the examining table. "Sit here."

Patrick staggered over and almost missed the table while sitting. He had to steady himself as Mara fetched a basin of water, soap, and a strip of clean linen. The stench of cheap whisky made Mara jerk her head away to avert his breath. She turned to inhale fresh air before facing him again. "Try to sit still." She dabbed the swelling around the eye, wiping away the blood and pus with brisk, careful strokes. "That looks better. She walked over to the cupboard, got a bottle of antiseptic, and a clean cloth. "This may sting." She moistened the cloth with antiseptic and laid it over his eye. Hold it there."

Patrick held the cloth to his eye.

"It will help reduce the swelling, but I'm afraid it won't be perfect before your Sunday service."

Patrick leaned back and pressed the cloth harder. "About Sunday's service…I should have said this sooner. I am sorry about your father. Reverend Sutcliff was an outstanding man and minister. My words aren't much," he lowered the medicated cloth from his bruised eye, "but I am sorry. Miss Sutcliffe, we still don't have a piano player. Yet Sunday's service would be blessed if you would sing *Amazing Grace* a capella in your father's honor."

"My mother led the chapel music before you arrived, Reverend Kiernan. She played the piano during our services. I can't play as well as she does, but she taught me. I can play piano and sing."

"You must miss your mother."

"Yes, Reverend Kiernan. I miss her with all my heart. She lives in Calcutta, and my father lives in Heaven. I have accepted my responsibility for God's judgment." Mara bowed her head. "Yes… I am ready to play piano and sing for the congregation."

"I see no need for us to drag the piano from the school to the chapel. K.K. would never approve of you playing in the chapel. Besides, your voice is too beautiful for an old piano. I want you standing front and center on the chancel and glorifying God with your voice alone."

"Won't Mrs. Kiernan object?"

"Of course she will." Patrick hiccupped. "She fancies herself as a pianist, and sometimes she sings, but she's not very…" He wiped a whisky-laden sweat bead from his brow. "We will keep this our secret."

"I believe God wants me to accept your invitation." She lifted her gaze and half smiled. "And I will remember Karen when I sing." She tapped Patrick's tight hand.

A solitary tear slid from Reverend Kiernan's good eye.

Kathleen was spying through a window. She pressed her arms tight against her sides and clenched her fists.

Chapter 27

Corporal Stanton rode over to Lawrence, who was viewing the worksite through his theodolite. "Lawrence! I'm so sorry. Amanda told me the terrible news." Douglas tipped his pith helmet. "We are all sad, but you have my deepest condolences, and please give my sympathies to Mara."

"Thank you, Douglas." Lawrence kept his eye on the theodolite lens. "He was like a second father to me. Mara is taking it hard, and her mother even harder. Mara's blaming herself. I wish I could reach her. I can't convince her that she has no power over mindless reptiles."

The Corporal swung off his horse and walked over to Lawrence. "Mindless reptiles? That's the official police report. I'm not buying it. An Assamese constable earns in a month what I make in a week and what you likely make in a day. For the right handful of rupees, their eyes tend to look the other way. People are vanishing. They barely lifted a finger over the attempt on your life, and my superiors signed off on my shooting a man without so much as a question."

"What are you trying to say?" Lawrence lifted his eye from his theodolite.

"I'm saying someone with power and money is up to something. But who are we to know?" He spread his hands. "I'm just a soldier, and you're a railway engineer. Still, there is some good news among the bad." Douglas's smile was small but genuine. "Amanda was in tears when she told me about Mara's father. I put my arms around her, and she held me even tighter. When I gazed into her big, teary eyes, I couldn't help myself. I asked her to marry me," Douglas beamed. "She said yes."

"Let me say it, Blimey!" Lawrence chuckled. "And Congratulations." He shook Douglas's hand. "Amanda is a wonderful woman, and she will make a great wife. What are your plans?"

"Well, the Army is returning me to England as soon as the railway reaches Chittagong. As it is, I have just six months left on my enlistment. They're also sending Amanda back soon. She'll work in a London hospital. I've got my railway job waiting for me, but I'm going to go to school in my spare time to learn engineering and drafting. I want to be the man designing the engines instead of just shoveling coal into them." Douglas mounted his horse. "How about you and Mara? You gotta come and visit us in England."

"Yeah," Lawrence peered into his theodolite and then jotted his findings into a notepad. He glanced at Douglas, "I'll leave everything in God's hands."

***

Lawrence arrived at his Dak Bungalow room. He put his felt, wide-brimmed hat onto a dressing table and pulled off his sweat-soaked bandana.

An item waiting on his pillow stopped him cold. The envelope was pink with American stamps marching from the right corner toward the center. He lifted it to his nose; it carried her favorite perfume. The return address read: Wayne, Pennsylvania, USA. Above it was the name Dorothy Cabot. He closed his eyes and silently prayed, *Oh, Lord, give me strength.* He carefully opened the envelope and began to read.

Dearest Lawrence,

It's been almost a year since the saddest day of my life. And no, my saddest day was not standing on the pier in New York, waving goodbye as the RMS Oceanic carried you from my arms. No, Lawrence. My worst day was sitting with my father and writing that dreadful letter ending our engagement.

Will you believe me when I tell you it was never my choice?

Please understand that I've lived my whole life beneath my father's wing. He has only ever sought what he believes is best for the family and for me. Over the last year, he arranged calls and dinners with eligible young men from prominent families. Yet not one of them appealed to me, for I could think of only you.

My father has received letters about you from India. Sir Nigel Browning, the great tea tycoon, Fredrick Robert Upcott, Chairman of the Railway Board, and even Prince Alaric of Schwatzenheim have all written in your praise. Because of these letters, my father has changed his mind about you. He now wants to take you under his wing and teach you everything he knows about banking. He has already begun looking for a house for us.

I love you, Lawrence. I never ceased loving you.

My father has already cleared the way with the Railway Board to release you from your contract and let you come home. Simply send my father a wire, and he will arrange your passage. Before long, I shall be standing on the New York pier, waiting for you with open arms and kisses upon my lips.

Love,

Dorothy

Lawrence collapsed on his bed and stared at the ceiling. He pressed Dorothy's letter to his chest and shut his eyes. *Lord, what shall I do?*

Chapter 28

Mara swept the chapel floor with a push broom. Kathleen burst through the door.

"When are you going to finish? The service is tomorrow morning, and my chapel looks like a pigsty. Look at that," she jabbed her finger toward a thin line of dust, "you missed a spot. You may be used to sweeping sawdust off the floors of dockside bars, but this is a church." She planted her hands on her hips and jutted her jaw. "You have no way of knowing this, but cleanliness is next to Godliness." Her gaze raked Mara up and down. "Ugh." She grunted and marched out of the chapel.

Mara sat on a pew and prayed, "Lord Jesus, David failed and fled to a cave, yet you sustained him. Please grant me that same patience and strength. Amen."

***

Sunday morning. Patrick Kiernan missed the chancel step and lurched forward, bracing himself on the pulpit. He cleared his throat twice. Brethren, and, ah, sisters, we are gathered, um, we are gathered, aren't we?"

A thin, uncertain chuckle rippled through the pews.

"Yes," he nodded, gripping the sides of the pulpit. "We are gathered in the house of the Lord. And the Lord… He is most obliging. He stands at the door and knocks." Reverend Kiernan hiccupped. "And when we let him in, he is gathered here with us. Jesus said, also Paul, and I think Peter too, that he will come like a thief in the night, so be watchful. You don't know when he will return. And when he does, you want him to take you up to Heaven. So, don't live in sin. Be doing good when he comes calling. He recently called your Pastor home. Reverend Sutcliffe was a good man, but now, now, I am called to stand in his place.

You didn't just lose a pastor; Miss Mara lost her father." His voice cracked. "And several years ago, I lost…I lost…I lost my child." Reverend Kiernan's words crumbled. He bowed his head over the pulpit and broke down.

Mara briskly strode in front of him and sang, "Amazing Grace, how sweet the sound that saved a wretch like me…" Her perfect pitch and clear, vibrato-free voice filled the chapel and rose to the rafters. By the second line, every eye had turned from the broken man at the pulpit to the young woman standing before him. Mara felt her shoulders loosen; her singing had pulled the weight of the moment off Reverend Kiernan. She put her heart into the remaining verses.

After she finished, the congregation sat in stunned silence. One man stood and applauded. Another followed, then another, until the whole chapel was on its feet applauding.

Reverend Kiernan raised his head. His eyes were red, but he managed a wavering smile. "I…I thank you, Miss Mara. Now, may the Lord who heals the sick, raises the dead, and turns the water into wine, bless you and keep you, and may he shine upon you." Patrick stepped down from the pulpit and staggered halfway down the aisle. He steadied himself by grabbing the edge of a pew before making it all the way up the aisle. Kathleen waited stiffly at the Chapel entrance.

Mara had tried to slip out the side exit, but the congregation surrounded her before she could reach the door. No one went forward to greet Patrick and Kathleen.

Kathleen glowered, huffed, and charged down the aisle like a rhino. She shoved through the cluster around Mara. "You little trollop! This is the Lord's house, not the Crazy Horse Saloon. How dare you wear that shameless blue dress when singing a sacred hymn?"

The congregants surged between them, separating Mara from Kathlene. They shouted at her in Assamese.

Chapter 29

Mara waited in the telegraph office, surrounded by ink stains, dust, and the dry tick of the telegraph sounder.

"Here it is, madam." The clerk held up a thin telegraph slip.

Mara took the note, thanked him, and read it. A true smile touched her face for the first time since she tumbled down the hill in Lawrence's arms, before their kisses had crossed from innocence to desire.

Mara clutched the telegram and marched home. She heard children in the schoolhouse. *Why are they there? I told their parents that class would not be in session until next Monday.* Mara walked inside and blanched. At the front of the room, Kathleen was teaching the children.

Kathleen tapped on a boy's desk with a pointer. "Arun. What's six times zero?"

"Six," the young boy squeaked.

"No! Any number multiplied by zero is zero." She smacked the desk with her pointer. "What is six times one?"

"Zero," Arun blushed and lowered until his chin almost touched the desktop.

"Stand up." Kathleen leveled the pointer at him. Arun jittered as he rose. "Turn around!" Kathleen whacked his buttocks with her pointer.

Arun shrieked and burst into tears.

"Stop your blubbering and sit down." Kathleen planted her hands on her hips. "Anyone else wish to daydream through my class?"

Mara lurched forward, snatched the pointer, snapped it over her knee, and flung the halves into the corner. Mara squared her shoulders and glared at Kathleen.

Kathleen slumped. Mara now towered over her. For an instant, she saw her grandfather, a cane in his hand and malice in his eyes.

Mara pulled the telegram from her pocket. "This is from the Baptist Missions Board. Yes. The house and chapel are yours. My father established the school and dispensary." Mara shoved the telegram into Kathlene's right hand. "As you can see, they're mine. I've moved my belongings to the clinic. I live there now. You can cook your own meals and clean up after yourself." Mara jabbed her finger toward the door. "Now get out and don't ever set foot in here again."

Kathleen's jaw chattered. She felt a weight press down on her shoulder, a warm breath in her ear, and a voice in her head. *Hit her…Hit her.* Kathleen's nervous hand shot out and slapped Mara's right cheek.

Mara neither flinched nor changed her expression. She turned her left cheek to Kathleen.

Kathleen took a step back.

Mara's gaze stayed fixed on her, hard and tight as telegraph wire.

Kathleen lost control of her bladder. The urine flow darkened her dress and pattered to the floor, pooling at her feet.

The children laughed.

Kathleen whirled toward them. They guffawed. Some stood, clutching their bellies as they howled. Their mocking faces seemed to wheel around her like windmill blades. She turned and fled from the schoolhouse.

Kathleen wandered down Sundarpur's main street in a daze. She lost all sense of distance, finally stopping by the bazaar to catch her breath. Only now did she realize that she was drenched in sweat. A gust blew dust into the rivulets of sweat running down her porcine cheeks. She wiped her eyes and found herself facing a man wearing a white dhoti and turban, seated before two wicker baskets and playing a tune on a reed pipe. A cobra rose from the nearest basket, hood flared. A second cobra followed. Instead of swaying to the snake charmer's head movements, they slid to Kathleen and coiled around her leg, their bodies winding upward until their hoods hovered before her eyes. Rather than terror, she sensed a strange, inexplicable kinship.

The snake charmer stood and walked over, mouth hanging open. "Memsahib! They like you!" The man rapped the ground with his staff and extended it toward Katheen. The snakes slithered onto his staff. He carried them to his baskets and dropped them back inside.

***

Mara embarked on the long walk to her favorite hill. At the summit, she paused, taking in the wide sweep of jungle and the distant gleam of the Brahmaputra River. Lawrence filled her thoughts with their ecstatic tumble down the slope, their lips locked and arms entwined. The memory of what happened at the bottom sent a tingle through her and raised gooseflesh along her arms. "No. No." She closed her eyes and prayed. "Lord Jesus, in the name of the Father, I accept your judgment. My father is gone; Lawrence is gone. Please forgive me and guide me to serve you for the rest of my days. Amen." Mara squeezed her eyelids shut to withhold her tears. She first inhaled the scent of a flower garden, unlike any fragrance in India. A soft hand touched her shoulder; an effulgence flooded her eyes. She looked up and saw a mind-boggling sight.

The woman before her had great wings of thick, dazzling white plumage that matched the V-cut sweep of her gown. Her figure was graceful, her beauty serene rather than earthly. Blue eyes, clear as cut sapphires, met Mara's. Indigo hair fell over your shoulders like a waterfall. Her full mouth curved into a luminous smile. "Mara, Heaven has heard your every prayer. Don't fret, Mara. You are a blessed child of God, still growing in the spirit. Remember reading the holy word with your mother? That you are not to grieve like those who have no hope. Yet you pray as if you had none."

"Who are you?" Mara took a deep breath. "You are so beautiful. You're gorgeous beyond what even a great artist could paint. I am a believer. I have hope that I will see my father again in Heaven. Why do you doubt my faith?"

"I am Isolde Maria. I am a Heavenly Angel. The angels were created in an order above mankind, but you are blessed among humans. I am here to guide you, Mara. I do not doubt your faith; yet your faith is misdirected. Unbelievers link separate, unrelated events and call it a divine pattern, as if it must forever remain so. Your father was not taken because you sinned with Lawrence. Yes. You lost yourself in desire, but it was born of love. You stopped yourself and repented. You never had to end your courtship with Lawrence. That was your choice. Mara, your father was not taken because of God's judgment of you. An unrelated act of evil took your father. Evil came into being before the Fall in the Garden of Eden. At the final hour, our Heavenly Father will banish evil forever. Until that day, man has a free will to choose good or evil."

"But crocodiles?" Mara asked. "They're not evil. They're just animals acting on instinct."

"Oh, Mara, my precious, beautiful child. Only after the final trumpet will the lion lie with the lamb. Soon you will learn that crocodiles did not kill your father. Some things are to remain a mystery until you join the angels in Heaven. You shall soon be tested. Perhaps, beyond what you can bear. A horrible evil is taking lives and even souls. It is poised to take many more. If you can overcome and endure to the end, that evil will be stopped.”

“I don’t understand Isolde Maria.”

“Soon you will, Mara.” The angel smiled. “Have faith in God’s plan. He loves you more than you can know on this earthly shore. And I love you, Mara.” Isolde Maria rested her hands on Mara’s shoulders; her delicate fingers slid up to cup her cheeks. She bent and brushed a soft, lingering peck upon Mara’s lips. For a heartbeat, warmth shimmered through Mara’s being before lifting, clean and bright, the light pouring into her soul. “I love you, Mara. I love you as only an angel can love. May our Heavenly Father bless you.” The angel vanished, leaving behind only a lingering floral fragrance. Mara smiled. *I have been kissed and blessed by one of God’s angels. If God be for me, who can be against me?*

Mara walked home on the trail with renewed resolve. Two men in black dhotis with red kamarbands sprang from the thicket. One clamped an arm across her chest and slapped his hand over her mouth while the other grabbed her ankles. Together they rushed her to the main road and flung her into a waiting carriage.

Chapter 30

The shock of her rough abduction ebbed. Mara silently prayed, Lord, let the blessing you gave me through your angel strengthen me. Calm me and help me to hold my tongue. She took a deep breath and steeled herself. I have no choice. I must face him. The intensity of his gaze opened a window onto the terror within. The lust in his face promised worse to come.

"Welcome, Mara." Nigel Browning crossed his right ankle over his thigh and laced his fingers together over his knee. "I apologize for the brusqueness of my hired help. They don't even know how to handle a woman, much less a Goddess."

Mara remained silent and still.

"You're quiet. That's step one. Nevertheless, I didn't expect you to thrash and scream." Sir Nigel leaned forward. "Not only would it be beneath you, but you're also clever enough to know that it would do you no good. Besides, we have a lifetime to converse." He sat back and folded his hands behind his head. "An eternity, actually."

Mara kept her face utterly still.

"I can tell that Mara hates me. That is irrelevant, for soon Mara will cease to exist. As we get to know each other," he paused for effect, "Intimately." The corners of his mouth slowly rose. "The Goddess inside of you will awaken. You will fulfill your destiny as Kali, and our union will awaken my inner Shiva. Together we will destroy, recreate, and rule. As you can hear from the hooves, you will soon arrive at your new home. You will share my empire with me. Our children will inherit more than a great tea plantation, Mara. They will inherit the world and everything in it."

Mara refused to flinch or even blink. Lord Jesus, I know you are with me. She prayed. Strengthen me. She squeezed her eyes shut and gritted her teeth. Strengthen me. Let me not shame your name. Use me to stop this evil. If I must die, let me die faithful, and comfort and protect the loved ones I leave behind.

***

Sir Nigel Browning led Mara down the main hallway of his mansion. Mara looked at his hunting trophies mounted along the wall. Their glass eyes seemed to glisten with pity, as if they shed a silent tear for her.

"You have been here before." Browning faced Mara. "Let me show you the rest of your home."

Browning opened a door at the end of the corridor. "This is our master bedroom." He stepped aside and gestured toward the bed, an imposing four-poster of dark, carved oak. Heavy posts rose at each corner, coiled like serpents, supporting a canopy draped in deep crimson fabric. The coverlet was a spread of rich, wine-red silk edged with gold fringe, and two bolsters lay across it like offerings before an altar. "Here is the bed where we shall share our marital bliss."

Mara blanched.

"I know what you are thinking." Browning lifted his right hand. "I can have you now, whenever I please, and at my pleasure. No, Kali, I will wait. A Goddess must come to her altar untouched. Three nights from now, you shall stand on our Temple chancel and receive your first worship. They will bow before you as a virgin, radiant in the purity of a blessed Goddess who has never known a man. We will share wedding vows. You will then arise as Kali and belong to me, soon giving me your body and soul in the ultimate intimacy. That will have to wait until our wedding night. Until then, permit me to show you to your temporary quarters."

***

Sir Nigel led Mara to the rear door of the manor. The heavy latch clanged as he drew it back. He stepped aside and waited for her to go first. She gasped. Set apart from the manor, the temple's walls gleamed in the sun; its high, narrow roofline spearing upward like a spire, every corner cutting at the sky. A spiked wrought-iron fence encircled the grounds. Sir Nigel opened the broad gate and gestured her through.

Mara trembled. I've lived my entire life among Hindu temples. They were just buildings. Yet this place crawls with demons. She followed a wide path among Serpents coiled at a god's feet and a purple goddess sitting astride a tiger, figures posed like courtiers awaiting judgment. Why do I sense that those lumps of clay and porcelain hate me?

Browning opened the door to the temple building. Mara froze on the threshold. He shoved her through the door. She stumbled inside. "I apologize for my discourtesy. I see the Mara within you remains strong. I trust that will be the last time I must respond to your stubbornness with conduct falling short of a gentleman. Surely, I will need only gentleness after Kali takes your soul as her rightful possession and submits to me as her husband and her God, Shiva.

He led her down a narrow stairway. Wall-mounted torches cast macabre shadows that writhed along the bare walls. At the bottom, he brought her to a life-sized figure draped in silk. Browning narrowed his eyes and grinned. "Behold!" He whisked away the covering. The statue beneath mirrored her every detail. Mara gasped and covered her face.

"At last, you react," Browning raised his hands. "You have hidden behind that little stoicism in defiance. She is you, and you are her. Kali. Goddess of destruction, renewal, and rule. Soon, you will be as one with Kali as you shall be as one with me, Shiva. Understand this," Browning pursed his lips, "Consequences remain for you as Mara if you defy me. Our stepson, Skanda, will conduct our wedding ceremony. Should you refuse to speak your vows, or resist the joy of our marital bed afterward, your body as Mara will be set alight with burning oil. While your body burns, your soul will pass into the idol, and it will quicken into your new divine body as Kali. The end will be the same as if you had cooperated, only this time your flesh will suffer the pain of fire."

A cold tear tracked down Mara's cheek.

"Ahh," Browning raised his hands and beamed. "We have company. Introducing Mr. Marco Bellini, the man whose divinely guided hands created your embodiment."

Marco Bellini gasped at the sight of Mara standing beside the statue. He dropped to the floor prostrate before her. "Kali, Kali, blessed thee. Kali, Kali, blessed thee. Kali, Kali, blessed thee." He continued to murmur, turning it into a mantra.

Sir Nigel's fingers brushed Mara's arm. She jerked her shoulder away from his touch. He gave a soft snigger. "How does it feel to be worshiped? Soon, thousands- millions- will bow their heads to you. Our devoted Mr. Bellini will mold thousands of these. They will be placed in temples across the globe. For you are Kali. You are a Goddess."

***

"I apologize, as a titled gentleman, that your temporary quarters are unfit for either a goddess or my future wife." Browning had escorted Mara to a windowless, whitewashed room with only a bed, a chair, and a small table with a pitcher of water. "Three nights from now, you will co-own my entire estate and soon after, the entire world and everything in it. But first, before Kali rises from within you, I must keep you from the sun. Your skin must be porcelain white, reflecting the purity of Mara and the soul that shall mingle with Kali. Many will attend our wedding. All know that the white races are mentally, biologically, and culturally superior to the dark races. I will not see you until our

180

wedding." Browning leaned in to kiss her. Mara shoved him away. "So be it- for now." He wagged his finger at her. "Do not forget the cost of defying me on the altar or in the bed afterwards." Browning left the room and locked the door behind him.

Mara dropped to her knees and began to sing hymns.

***

Mara refused to eat. She spent the next three days praying and singing hymns. Lord Jesus, in the name of the Father, if it be your will that my flesh suffer death by fire, I submit. May the agony be short-lasting, for I know the glory of Heaven is forever. May my death glorify you. Please comfort my mother, Leena, let her know I did not die in vain. Tell Lawrence that I'm sorry and that I never ceased loving him. In the name of the Father, the Son, and the Holy Ghost. Amen.

Mara heard tinkling bells before hearing the scrape of a key in the lock and the creak of the door opening. Anjali entered with a white gown draped over her arm. Layla set a basin with a sponge, bar of soap, and a small box of cosmetics on the bedside table. She emptied the basin and filled it with water from the pitcher. Both were barefoot, anklets chiming with each step. Their saris were sheer and clinging, cut bare to their midriffs and shoulders. Layla wore an emerald-green choli; Anjali's choli was ruby red.

Brahman stood outside the doorway, wearing a black turban and a black dhoti. His red kamarband was embroidered with gold leaves. Two large Assamese men flanked him, also in black dhotis, except their kamarbands were plain red.

"Your wedding is at hand." Anjali carefully folded the white gown over the back of the chair.

Layla moved close enough that her shoulder touched Mara's. "We're here to wash you and dress you."

181

Mara blanched.

"We remember how you looked at us when we first met." Anjali laid her hand on Mara's shoulder.

Mara flinched.

"Mara, let us prepare you," Layla tipped her head toward the door. "Or they will."

A single tear slipped down Mara's cheek as she nodded.

Anjali turned to Brahman and nodded. He swung the door shut and turned the key.

"I'll speak plain, Mara." Layla gave a crooked little smile. "We do look forward to seeing you without your clothes. But do not fear, Sir Nigel would burn us alive if we touch you wrongly." Layla gasped. The last words flew from her mouth before she could catch them. She clamped a hand to her mouth.

Anjali seized Layla's arm and gave it a sharp tug. "What she means is…" Anjali shut her eyes and bit her lip. "…He would have us doused in oil and set alight if we cross him. He sees you as a Goddess. Defiling you would be the ultimate sin in his eyes."

Layla drew a long breath. "I know you think of us as a pair of fallen whores who lie with their own kind, but in truth, we are like you. We are all Sir Nigel's prisoners." She raised her bare foot, the bells at her ankle chiming. "He will not suffer us to wear shoes, and he fastened these bells on us so he can always hear where we are."

"Anjali, Layla, I don't see you the way you think I do. I see you as Jesus sees us all, poor sinners in need of grace."

"Sinners in need of grace?" Anjali sniggered. "That's rich, coming from the goddess of purity."

"No, Anjali," Mara lifted both hands. "That Goddess talk is Sir Nigel's depravity, not truth. I am as fallen as any soul. All have sinned and fallen short of God's glory. Jesus died for my sins, and he died for yours as well." A faint smile touched her mouth. "Jesus loves you."

"Love? What's love?" Layla spread her hands. "We saw you with your parents. Anyone could see they loved you. Ours sold us to Sir Nigel as if we were sacks of rice. Love? The only love left to us is our love for one another, and he permits us only because it amuses him."

"Each time he forces us to lie with him; each time he sends us to lie with one of his friends, a part of us dies. All we have is each other." Anjali embraced Layla and kissed her lips. "In just a few hours, his touch will sicken you, too. We love you, Mara. Soon we will endure our lives together."

Moisture filled Mara's eyes. "I love you both. I love you as Jesus loves you. I want us together in Heaven when this life is past. But we shall not remain together on this shore."

"How can your God receive us in his Heaven after all the filth we've been dragged through?" Layla's tears spilled. "We are defiled past mending."

"No, Layla," Mara stepped nearer. "Jesus received a sinful woman and let her wash his feet with her tears. He saved an adulteress from stoning. He sat and spoke with a shunned woman at the well. He washes away all sin with his blood. He died for us all."

"Oh, Mara, we do love you." Anjali pressed her hands together and bowed her head. "Please do what Sir Nigel bids. We cannot bear to see you burned. What sin could be worse than letting your face and body be turned to ash? And he will do it." Her breath came fast. "We have seen his rites. He sends his men in black dhotis and red kamarbands to seize whomever they can. He cuts them with his dagger and splashes their blood on his idol of Kali. He believes that their blood will rouse her. Now that he has found you, he's convinced his goddess has arrived. He has burned to death anyone who blasphemes her or who defies him."

Layla met Anjali's gaze. Anjali gave a small nod. "Mara, we were there. Sir Nigel slew your father and splashed his blood on the statue that bears your image."

Mara's heart palpitated. She fought back bile.

Anjali set her hands on Mara's shoulders. "For all Sir Nigel did to shame and defile your father, I can tell you this, he met death bravely and held fast to his faith."

Mara's breath hitched. Sweat and tears mingled on her cheeks. "Layla, Anjali, Jesus endured an excruciating death for me. Now I see it clearly." Mara bowed her head. "I am called to die for him, just as Brian faced death for his faith. It is the only way Sir Nigel's madness ends."

"You mean, you love this Jesus so much that you would suffer burning alive for him?" Anjali, astonished, raised her hands.

"Yes." Mara's voice steadied. "I know I must."

"We want what you have." Layla dropped to one knee and gazed up at Mara with moist eyes. "How can we know Jesus?"

"Are you earnest? Will you turn from this life and trust in him?"

"Yes. We are earnest." Anjali and Layla nodded at each other. "And yes, we will turn from this life and trust in him."

Mara laid a hand on each of their shoulders. "Do you repent of your sins and accept Christ Jesus's forgiveness? And do you take him into your hearts?"

"Yes, I do." Layla closed her eyes and bowed. "Lord Jesus, forgive me, take me as I am, cleanse me of my sins, and come into my heart. Save me."

Anjali knelt beside her. "Yes. Lord Jesus. Forgive my sins. Have mercy upon me. Save me, come into my heart, and make me yours."

"The Lord has heard you and answered your prayers. You are both now new creations." Mara placed her hands on their heads. "You no longer belong to Sir Nigel. Listen, Sir Nigel and his men will all be fixated on the wedding. You don't have to turn from this life by facing death by fire. My being burned alive will cause a huge commotion. That will be your chance to escape."

"Where can we go?" Anjali stood.

"Just go. Go as far away as your feet can carry you. Have faith that God will lead you. You are precious in his eyes and in my eyes. You must not let Sir Nigel defile you any further." Mara took a deep breath. "Until then," Mara lifted the gown from the chair and placed it in Anjali's hands. "Do what you must. This is not the hour to flee."

***

"We've never dreamt anything could be so lovely." Anjali stepped back and looked Mara up and down in the gown. It was white and unadorned save for a narrow border of embroidery at the hem. The skirt fell in soft folds around her ankles like a pale echo of a bridal sari. "And your face, Layla, has made a masterpiece of it."

Anjali grinned, "I wish you had black leather shoes with spikes to match, but Sir Nigel wants you barefoot."

"No! Mara! No!" Layla cried out. "We don't want you to be burned to death." She sobbed, pressing the hem of Mara's gown to her eyes.

"I don't want to die either." Mara burst into tears. "But I must."

Anjali collapsed onto her knees, buried her face into the gown, and wept with her.

Mara threaded her fingers through their hair and pulled their faces deeper into the gown's hem until their brows rested against her legs. Their tears fell as one upon the white cloth. Footsteps sounded in the hallway. "They're coming," Mara said quietly. "Stand up. We must dry our eyes. It is time to do what we must." She set her hands on Layla's shoulders. "Good-bye, Layla." She brushed a quick kiss on Layla's lips, then did the same for Anjali.

The footsteps halted outside the door.

Chapter 31

Layla and Anjali stood back as two Assamese men in black dhotis with red kamarbands led Mara to a platform slung with pullies and ropes. Layla and Anjali dared not move; one careless step and their ankle bells would betray them to Browning's thugs. Brahman had ordered them to bear the gown's train, but when they saw that the lesser men paid them no heed, they stayed back and let it trail.

Mara stepped onto the platform.   She wiped away a tear and dared a final trembling wave.

***

"Kali, Kali, blessed thee. Shiva, Shiva, death and night and blood." The Temple congregation chanted. Four oil lamps on iron stands cast flickering light and shadows across their faces. Browning stood robed as a bridegroom for the goddess. He wore a long black silk coat, its hem and cuffs embroidered with licking gold flames. A crimson kamarband circled his waist. He had oiled and combed back his dark hair, hiding the gray at its tips. To his left loomed the statue of Mara as Kali.

Prince Alaric of Schwatzenheim, arrayed as Skanda in a smoke-gray robe embroidered with orange flames, stood before them. He raised his arms. "Silence! Your destiny draweth nigh. Kali shall rise and wed Sir Nigel.   Our leader shall ascend to godhood as Shiva. We shall gain immortality and command powers such as the world has never seen   After we destroy, we shall renew and rule the world and the Heavens above with Kali and Shiva." He lowered his arms.

The congregation roared back, "Kali, Kali, blessed thee. Shiva, Shiva, death and night and blood."

Two assistants pushed down on plungers. Thick smoke billowed over the chancel. Below, the thugs pulled the ropes, lowering the statue and raising the platform with Mara.

When the smoke parted, the idol had vanished. Mara now stood at Browning's right hand.

The chanting grew wild. "Kali, Kali, blessed thee! Kali, Kali, blessed thee! Kali, Kali, blessed thee!"

The prince flung his arms up once more. "Silence. Kneel in reverence and let our ceremony begin." He turned to Browning. "Do you, Sir Nigel, as Shiva incarnate, take Mara, our Kali, to be your wife, united in power and glory, and to rule the Earth forever?"

***

After the men finished hoisting the platform bearing Mara up to the temple chancel, they climbed the near stairway to join the worshippers.

Anjali turned to Layla and gripped her shoulders. "This is it." They embraced and brushed a quick kiss on each other's lips. Anjali drew back. "We have no time." Their ankle bells chiming, they ran for the far stairway and slipped out of the building.

***

"I do." Browning beamed at Mara, his victorious smile brightening, lust sharpening his gaze.

Prince Alaric turned to Mara. "Do you, Mara, as Kali incarnate, take Sir Nigel, our Shiva, to be your husband, united in power and glory, and to rule the Earth forever?"

The Temple fell into a dead, waiting silence.

Mara sang,

> *"You only live once, on this earthly shore,*
>
> *Your soul is a treasure, worth so much more.*
>
> *Though sorrows may stay, and years drift away,*
>
> *One Savior has come to show you the way."*

The worshipers gasped, then began to murmur. Browning twisted his lips grotesquely downward. He furrowed his brow into tight grooves. His fists clenched; his eyes flared.

Mara kept singing,

> *"One life, then eternity,*
>
> *The cross has won our victory.*
>
> *Rejoice, he has paid the price,*
>
> *No second death, but eternal life."*

Browning saw the shock and confusion on the worshippers' faces. "She blasphemes! Her mortal flesh denies the goddess! Let fire consume her corrupt body and let her soul rise as Kali."

Mara sang on,

> *"He calls the lost, through the darkest night,*
>
> *His mercy is strong; his love shines bright.*
>
> *The gate is narrow, but the shepherd will guide,*
>
> *His word shows the way; his arms open wide."*

Browning snatched up a flaming oil lamp and swung it at Mara like American baseballer Honus Wagner at bat. The flaming tip snapped off and flew into the crowd. It struck Brahman and set him ablaze. Burning oil splashed over three others and kindled their clothes. They screamed and flailed; the flames leapt to four more. In the panic, two floor lamps toppled. Fire raced up the walls. Ceiling lamps caught, the overhead punkah fans rained fire down upon the chancel. "I am Shiva!" Browning shrieked. "I command you flames to stop!"

The flames ignored him. The temple blazed.

The train and bodice of Mara's gown caught fire. Heat slathered her, yet instead of agony, multi-colored lights comforted her. She lifted her face and sang as the brilliance seemed to draw her upward.

"One life, then eternity,

The cross has won our victory.

Rejoice, he has paid the price,

No second death, but eternal life."

"He calls the lost, through the darkest night,

His mercy is strong; his love shines bright.

The gate is narrow, but the shepherd will guide,

His word shows the way; his arms open wide."

"One life, then eternity,

The cross has won our victory.

Rejoice, he has paid the price,

No second death, but eternal life."

"When shadows falter, and dawn appears,

He'll banish all pain and dry all our tears.

A crown of life he will give to all who believe,

and life without end, his children receive."

***

Outside, rain lashed the compound. Layla stopped running and looked back at the burning temple. "No! Mara!" She fell to her knees. A lightning bolt, jagged as broken glass, lit her shrieking face.

"Layla!" Anjali hauled her up to her feet. "The whole temple is on fire. It cannot be only Mara. Jesus has given us hope. We must go back and save her." Anjali took Layla's hand and ran back to the temple.

A charred wall beam fell, tearing open a gap in the wall. Anjali and Layla stepped inside the breach. "Mara!" They cried together. "Mara! Run to us!"

Their shouts awakened Mara from her trance. The vision of light faded. She turned from the chancel and ran toward the gap.

"Kali! No! I do not permit you to go!" Browning hurled himself at her. He seized the burning train and bodice of her gown and yanked. Mara stumbled. With a ripping sound, the flaming train and bodice tore free and snapped back onto him. Fire leapt up his arms and chest. He rolled, flailed, and screamed. A burning ceiling beam crashed onto him, pinning him, ending his earthly agony in a burst of sparks and smoke.

Anjali clasped Mara's right hand while Layla gripped her left. "Don't look back! Just run! Run for your life!" The three women ran through the driving rain hand in hand. Fueled by adrenaline and fear, they reached the factory and warehouse. "The boxcar on the spur." Anjali gasped for breath and pointed. "I overheard the men say that the railway will take it away around dawn. Let's hide there and wait." The three exhausted and drenched women huddled in the boxcar.

Exhausted, drenched, and shaking, the three soot-laden women clambered into the empty boxcar. They huddled together in the dark, listening to the distant roar of the temple and the drum of rain upon the roof.

Chapter 32

Exhaustion pressed on them, but the recent trauma had left the three women too agitated to rest. They shivered in their soaked clothes, teeth chattering in the open chill. All through the night, Mara led Anjali and Layla in prayers of thanksgiving and for protection, stopping only to cough up tea dust.

At first light, they heard the distant chug and rattle of a steam locomotive. The sound swelled until the iron horse coupled with the boxcar. The jolt sent the women sprawling. Anjali shrieked in pain. Mara gathered her into her arms and kissed the top of her head. "Please don't cry. Someone may hear us."

Next came the clank of an iron pin dropping into the boxcar's coupling link. A man shouted in Assamese; the locomotive answered with an ear-splitting whistle. With a harsh jolt, the boxcar lurched forward, carrying the women away.

The boxcar rocked; the sacks of tea leaves thudded and shifted. Spent, the women huddled into a corner to pray. Mara murmured, "Let's be grateful that the load is tea and not metal or ore." She held Anjali and Layla close, using her body to shield them from shifting bales.

***

An Assamese brass band, the musicians all in white, stood ready by the platform. Lawrence sat in the bandstand with high-ranking local dignitaries, senior British and Assamese officials, and high ranking military officers beneath bunting of British, Assamese, and Indian colors. Vendors had set up tents and canopies to hawk clothing and refreshments.

Jugglers, snake charmers, and street musicians amused the growing crowd. Lawrence was the proudest of all. The festival celebrated the arrival of the first train over the line to the *Gauhati* docks. Railway chairman Robert Fredrick Upcott was believed to be riding in the locomotive.

A distant billow of smoke on the horizon preceded a long, echoing toot. The band struck up Elgar's Pomp and Circumstance March. The crowd cheered as the train drew closer. It slowed and came to a stop by the docks. A railway worker slid open the nearest boxcar door, peered inside, and shouted in Assamese for a doctor.

Nurse Amanda Fairleigh ordered the coachman to drive their horse-drawn ambulance to the boxcar. She stepped down and looked inside. Her jaw dropped. Nearly letting her medical bag slip from her hand, she saw a woman in a charred, frayed wedding gown kneeling on the floor. Face streaked with soot and tea dust, her arms were wrapped around two pallid women with blank eyes and chattering jaws. They were almost naked in torn, drenched, and clinging clothes. "Mara?"

"Amanda! God has answered prayer. I'm all right. Please help my sisters. They saved my life."

Nurse Fairleigh shouted to two young Assamese assistants who arrived a moment later. "Get me a canister of hot coffee, two dry towels, two towels soaked in hot water, two blankets, and two hospital gowns. Don't let anyone look inside this car."

"And get a pair of metal shears," Mara added.

Amanda snipped away what remained of Anjali and Layla's saris with a pair of surgical scissors. Mara held a mug of hot coffee to their lips while Amanda rubbed away the dirt, rainwater, and sweat with towels soaked in hot water, afterward drying their bodies with clean ones. She dabbed their worst cuts and abrasions with cotton wool soaked in spirits, murmuring an apology each time they flinched. Together, the two women eased Anjali and Layla into hospital gowns and then draped them in blankets.

"Drink some of this coffee, Mara." Amanda tapped her hand. "You fared better than your friends, but you've been through a great deal. You need something hot in you."

A male voice called from the doorway, out of sight. "I've got the metal shears."

"You can come in now," Amanda answered.

Mara took the shears. "There's something I need to do." She knelt and snipped the metal bands that held the bells to their ankles. "I'm going to put these under the train wheels so these diabolical things can be crushed into oblivion."

Seeing the commotion, Corporal Stanton spurred his horse toward the boxcar. He swung down and looked inside. "Amanda, how can I help?" He looked behind Amanda and gasped. "Mara! It can't be…"

"You can marvel over her later," Amanda cut in. "Gather four men and bring two stretchers from the ambulance. I'll ride with them to the British military hospital." Amanda grasped Mara's hand, "Ride with us. We need to examine you, clean you up, and get you situated."

A railway worker set portable steps at the boxcar entrance. Four Assamese men carried Layla and Anjali from the boxcar in stretchers and eased them into the ambulance. Mara walked out with Amanda, watching her feet as she descended the stairs.

Mara looked up and saw him.

"Mara?" His eyes widened in wonder.

Mara beamed. The pain and terror of the previous days lifted like mist in the sunlight. "Lawrence."

They ambled closer to one another and stopped. Breathless, their eyes sang sonnets. They fell into a tight embrace. "Mara!" Their first kiss was fierce and grateful, more prayer than pleasure. Lawrence laughed joyfully.

He swept her off her feet and twirled her. "I love you!" He
cradled her. Mara braced her hand on the back of his neck. They
kissed again, so deeply that Heaven itself found a new hymn.
People gathered around and cheered, breaking their spell.

"We'd better not get carried away here." Mara massaged the
back of his neck and smiled. "Let me go with Amanda, get cleaned
up and out of this infernal gown. That will give you time to go to
the market and buy me another one. Hire a carriage and pick me
up at the hospital. From there, we'll go to St. Joseph's Cathedral
and stand before Bishop Fregosi." Mara brushed a soft kiss on his
lips. "After we exchange our vows, we can get carried away. Far,
far away."

Epilogue

1910

Lawrence sipped sherry from a slender-stemmed glass in the Philadelphia Academy of Music's lobby behind the exclusive boxes. George Cabot approached. His wife, Diana, was on his arm. Dorothy and her husband, Dwight Wilcox, were close behind.

"I trust you'll attend our reception at the Union League after the concert. I want you to know that the president of the New York Central Railroad, William C. Brown, will be in attendance." George Cabot placed a firm hand on Lawrence's arm, leaned in, and lowered his voice. "I know your loyalty lies with the Pennsylvania Railroad. I would expect no less from a man of your caliber. My sources tell me Brown intends to make you a substantial offer to join him. Hear him out." He grinned, "and bargain him up. You needn't accept. I'll see that word reaches your president, James McCrea. It will surely impact your next raise."

"Well, I must say, Mr. Cabot…"

"George."

"George," Lawrence corrected with a chuckle. "When it comes to money, you play second fiddle to none. You're the business world's Niccolò Paganini. Advice taken and appreciated."

Dwight Wilcox, nearly Lawrence's height but thinner in his tailored coattails, joined in. "What did you think of the first half? I enjoyed the Lohengrin prelude, though Toscanini at the Met conducts it with more finesse. Still, when our Carl Pohlig struck the surprise chord in Haydn's *Surprise* Symphony, I nearly jumped from my seat."

Dorothy fluttered a lace hand fan before her face. "You, more than anyone, must be strung tighter than piano wire waiting for the second half. Once the orchestra begins, I imagine you'll want the first three movements to pass in a blur."

"I'm sure Lawrence will savor all of Mahler's *Third*," Diana Cabot added. "But yes, I know the fourth movement carries special meaning tonight."

"That it does," Lawrence beamed. "After all, this is her first appearance since Madame Mathilde Marchesi came from Paris to coach her."

The house lights flashed twice, summoning the audience.

"Well, this is it." Lawrence shook George's hand. "I'll see you at the Union League." He shook Dwight's hand next, then offered polite, quick pecks to Dorothy and Diana's cheeks.

Lawrence returned to his private box overlooking the stage. Leena had already brought back her grandchildren, four-year-old Brian and two-year-old Amanda.

"Daddy!" Brian stood eagerly.

"Now, little ones," he whispered, "you must stay quiet. This is Mommy's big night."

Lawrence lifted Brian; Leena hoisted Amanda. They joined the audience in applauding as Carl Pohlig took center stage. He acknowledged them, turned to the orchestra, and raised his baton.

***

The Academy of Music fell breathlessly silent after the last note of the third movement.

She entered.

Mara crossed the stage in a pale silver, empire-waist Edwardian gown shimmering with jeweled sequins that caught the gaslight like frost. The crowd rose as one and applauded. She waited— still, composed—until they settled.

The orchestra offered a soft F-major chord. Then A-minor. Low strings hovering, a single high A suspended above like a star.

On that pitch, Mara drew in a deep breath and sang,

"O Mensch! Gib Acht! Was spricht die tiefe Mitternacht?..."

She stunned the hall with the clarity, warmth, and depth of her voice. Her interpretation was luminous, personal, and prayerful.

The children's choir entered for the fifth movement, *What the Angels Tell Me*. Their four chiming *Bimm-Bamms* opened the piece. Mara joined them, her voice soaring above theirs. Leena leaned toward her grandchildren. "Someday you'll be on that stage, singing beside your mother."

Mara's performance prepared the hall for the sixth movement, *What Love Tells Me*, the vast, spiritual finale.

***

The Union League glittered with evening finery. Four members of Congress and two U.S. Senators were present. James McCrea of the Pennsylvania Railroad and William C. Brown of the New York Central spoke quietly near the fireplace. George Westinghouse and Andrew Carnegie stood beside them. Several men surrounded Connie Mack, owner and manager of the World Champion Philadelphia Athletics.

Leena, Brian, Amanda, and Lawrence waited outside the doors with Mara.

"Darling," Lawrence took both her hands, "you should walk in first. It's your night. We'll be right behind you."

Mara stepped through the doorway.

Conversation stopped.

The party burst into applause.

She glanced back. Her mother entered with Brian and Amanda; Lawrence brought up the rear. He moved beside her and held her hand.

Standing erect with his chin tilted upward and his shoulders back, he whispered in her ear, "I love you, Mara." He wrapped his arm around her waist, "on this earthly shore, and in Heaven forever more."